Robyn Warren farmed in West Dorset. He came from a family which had farmed in the area for many generations. He attended school until 1943, not a long period, but was then tutored by a university professor, which was a rewarding experience.

Having lived through the depression as a child, the war as a lad and various situations after, he then farmed his own farm for 18 years before moving to Nova Scotia with his wife, two sons and three collie dogs, in 1968.

Though Canada was a long way from family and friends, he set out to make a new life, always remembering the folks he left behind , the terror of the war and the sadness of personal tragedy.

SYRUP OF FIGS

Robyn Warren

Syrup Of Figs

Vanguard Press

A CIP catalogue record for this title is
available from the British Library
ISBN 1 903489 92 X

Vanguard Press is an imprint of
Pegasus Elliot MacKenzie Publishers Ltd.
www.pegasuspublishers.com

First Published in 2002

Vanguard Press
Sheraton House Castle Park
Cambridge England

Printed & Bound in Great Britain

Benjamin Carter was born on June 3rd 1927. He was a normal baby, born without difficulty. Ben's parents, Tom and Ellen Carter owned a chemist shop in the small seaside town of Midhampton, southern England. The main street ran east to west, another street ran due north from the wharf forming a crossroad at the centre of town. The church was on North Street.

The Church of England operated the church, which was bigger than the needs of the congregation. There were other smaller roads branching off the two main streets, north, south, east and west. There were several shops of all descriptions serving the townsfolk. The road to the wharf was fairly steep but easily negotiated.

The wharf was shaped like a horseshoe with two piers built out to sea, which almost met, but leaving the boats, which use the harbour, plenty of room. There is plenty of space in the harbour for the fishing boats and other boats belonging to people who use the harbour, especially at holiday times, when visitors would bring down their crafts. The harbour authority made sure that each boat would be accommodated to everyone's satisfaction.

Tom Carter owned a small boat he had purchased from a local fisherman a few years before Ben was born. With the purchase came the lobster traps in an area offshore with a rocky sea bottom that always seemed to be inhabited by lobsters.

In the main street of Midhampton is a fishmonger's shop, whose owner purchased fish and lobsters brought in by the local fishermen.

Tom Carter went fishing when he had time, and the

family, the surplus given away, used most of the catch. The fishermen never made fortunes but enough for a quite comfortable living, added to by taking visitors out in their boats for day trips.

Ben grew quickly and was soon taking an interest in what his parents were doing. Ben's grandmother lived in the cottage right next door to Tom's shop. She was delighted to have a grandson. Her name was Rose Ellen and her daughter was christened Ellen after her.

Rose was from a farm two miles north of Midhampton. Ben's grandfather has passed away several years before Ben was born. Rose always referred to him as 'my Charlie'.

Despite a great effort to run the farm herself after Charlie's passing, she found she just couldn't cope.

The farm was called 'Sweetwater Farm', named for the springs, which always ran water at all times. The farm had been in the family for many generations, and Rose was really heartbroken to have had to leave. She was especially proud of the large south Devon cattle the farm was famous for. The horses were sold too. They also gave Rose pleasure.

When Ben was born Rose's thoughts of Sweetwater Farm were not foremost in her mind. She had a grandson, and that meant so much to her.

When Ben was old enough he loved to help his father with the boat, and spent many hours trying to help but usually he got in the way. A lot of Ben's time was spent with his grandmother. When she left the farm she dug up the roses from her garden and brought them with her to her new home. The roses flourished and were a sight to behold. Rose cultivated the garden and grew vegetables for her own use, and for Tom and Ellen.

Ben soon developed an interest; he loved to help Rose in the garden, as much as working at the boat.

When the weather was fine Tom would take the boat up the coast to a beach only accessible from the sea; a picnic basket brought good things to eat, which Ben and his parents enjoyed.

Rose settled down to her new way of life, as opposite to the bustle and work of operating a farm as could be.

Tom, after much persuasion, agreed to set a few lobster traps for their own use, so every evening when the sea was not too rough Ben and Tom went see to their lobsters, and occasionally fished for, and caught other species of fish, again for the family's use.

When Tom was busy in the shop and the sea was calm Ben would take the boat out to the lobster traps, pull up any lobster traps caught, re-bait the traps and re-set them. He gradually became quite expert at handling the boat.

As Ben grew up the 12-foot boat became too small, and the outboard motor wouldn't last too much longer, so Tom decided to buy a larger boat.

He had heard of a suitable sized boat, but the inboard engine was in poor shape. There was a discussion with one of Tom's customers about an engineer and a very good mechanic who thought a new engine could easily be installed in the place of the old one. Tom thought about the project and eventually forgot about it, until one day Mr Walters, the mechanic, came into the store and said he had found an engine he thought would do. He explained that it was an engine from a Norton 500cc motorbike that had been in an accident, but which was almost new.

Tom inquired if anyone was hurt in the accident, and Mr Walters assured him that no one was. Tom agreed to go and see the battered motorbike, which certainly was a mess, except for the engine. So Tom agreed to buy it, then arranged for it to be towed home and replace the boat he presently owned.

Ben although only 8 years old helped where he could,

he sometimes got in the way, but eventually everything seemed to fit together.

The engine was bolted crossways so that the chain, which was used to drive the motorbike's back wheel, drove the shaft connected to the propeller that drove the boat. This proved to be a problem as the propeller was too large and the motor had to be cut to half speed.

New planks were added to each side of the boat, making it at least a foot higher. The throttle cable running to the carburettor was placed within reach of the rudders at the stern, so the person steering could handle both speed and direction.

The fuel tank from the motorbike had to be replaced as the original was destroyed in the accident.

Tom remembered there was a large can in his storeroom made of very tough metal. He also remembered the story about it. Many years ago a salesman came to the chemist shop and persuaded Tom to purchase 'Syrup of Figs' in a bulk container. Small bottles were bought at the same time as the five gallons of the syrup, which was supposed to be good for most ailments in those bygone years. The problem was that no one was buying too much, until one of Tom's customers remarked what a large quantity there was for sale. Tom said, without much thought, "it was supposed to be good for one's love life," whereupon the lady customer, having heard him, straight away bought two bottles, went home and told her neighbour about the elixir at the chemist shop. Soon word spread about the potential of Syrup of Figs and the bottles sold fast, which very soon emptied the five-gallon can.

The can was square and fitted well in the boat, above the engine. Someone had said they would paint it for Tom, but this was never done. 'Syrup of Figs' was printed on both sides of the can and remained there. Tom was teased, various remarks were made about the name, such as,

"Should run well," etc.

Ever after, the boat was referred to as *The Syrup of Figs*.

The family and many friends came for the launching of the boat. No one smashed a bottle or anything grand, but glasses of wine were raised and the *Syrup of Figs* was officially named and toasted. Then the boat was eased into the harbour. Ben pulled on the oars that were specially made for such a large boat, slowly taking her out into the centre of the harbour where, after a while, the Norton 500cc engine came to life, a bit noisy but powerful, and making a unique noise, despite the extra mufflers. Tom eased the throttle and the engine responded and went out of the harbour, perhaps a bit too fast, but the project proved to be a success.

****

Far away in the city of Leipzig in Germany, Sarah Benes was born at the same time as Ben Carter. Her parents owned a tailor's shop, which had always prospered because of the hard work and the quality of their workmanship.

The Benes' were Jewish, and got along very well with their customers, and anyone else for that matter.

Sarah grew up to be a very pretty girl with dark hair, light complexion and a happy disposition. She had been to school with other children, and was bright, happy and intelligent.

When the Nazi party came to power in Germany, with Hitler as Chancellor all things changed for the Benes family. Hitler ranted against the Jewish people inciting hatred from the non-Jewish population. Some of Sarah's young friends or people she thought were friends started making remarks about her being a Jew. At first Sarah didn't take much notice, children often call each other names. The day came when several children called her a 'Jew', and no longer would associate with her. Sarah was terribly upset, she thought being a German, was to be accepted as a German, but not as a Jew.

Sarah's parents David and Ruth Benes closed down their tailor's shop, and decided to take a short walk in the park, which was handy to their shop. David explained quietly to Ruth and Sarah, how he heard of Jewish people had had their lives threatened by the Germans.

"But we are Germans too," Ruth replied.

"But we are Jews even if we are German," said David.

Sarah's parents said no more on the subject, but Sarah knew they were worried. There lived a girl on the next street, who was Jewish too. She spoke English fluently as she had lived in England for a good deal of her life – first at school, then college. David asked her if she would teach his family English. At first she was suspicious, but eventually agreed to teach them, but only if, when they left Germany, they would take her with them. Her name was Rebecca. Her parents had died when she was a small girl, and she had been sent to live with relations in England. She returned to Germany after she finished her college education so that she could learn to speak German – what an irony.

From then on Rebecca insisted that the Benes' family spoke only in English in the confines of their own home. She explained it would be difficult to start with but would become easier for her to correct their English that way.

The Benes purchased cloth with their savings to be delivered to his uncle in London. This was not difficult as the material was made in England. This cloth was to be used by them if they ever escaped Germany and got to England.

David's uncle sent designs for English style clothes.

When they left they would change their names to Bennett. Somehow, David's uncle in England obtained British passports after receiving the necessary photos of the four. The Benes family worked tirelessly at speaking English, with effort overcoming the 'V' and 'W's.

Hitler ranted and raved at the Jewish people, some were arrested without reason, and were never seen again.

About this time, a rock was thrown through the tailor shop window, which was a terrifying experience.

The rounding up of the Jewish people had begun. The hatred incited by Hitler and his gang, without much effort, had the horrendous result, of turning a so-called civilized nation into murderers.

After the rocks were thrown through the window the family was terrified, especially Sarah. It was then that Mr Benes made the decision to leave Germany. He boarded up the broken window to prevent looters, and he knew it would be a short time until he too would be arrested. The thought of being parted from his wife and Sarah haunted his thoughts. He had heard of families being split up, never to see each other again.

David put up a sign on his window "Open for Business" so as not to give any impression that he was leaving. Germans, who David knew well, passed on the other side of the street, saying nothing. David thought perhaps they had always been hated. He walked back into the shop to tell his wife he had business to do in the next street, and off he went to the home of Rebecca. Her name Rebecca suited her. David didn't know why, but it did.

Knocking, not too loudly on the door, he waited for a reply. She came eventually, very worried. She thought she was going to be rounded up.

Rebecca invited David inside, but he refused. David asked her if she would like to come with them. They were going for a drive, or perhaps a picnic somewhere. Rebecca understood and said, "I'll try, but I may be busy." This was part of a pre-arranged plan they had made. They were leaving Germany, or hoped to. Rebecca continued, "I'll be around in 20 minutes to let you know if I am coming."

They didn't know if anyone overheard their conversation. David left for home, not hurrying. He stopped at a tailor's shop to see what the competition offered, which was normal, then he walked on home. Rebecca came as planned twenty minutes later.

Ruth and David had made clothes for them all from designs sent from England by David's uncle.

David's uncle advised them to wear English style clothes and to speak English, when in Germany. "If you leave, you are English people on holiday, and "wear the clothes often before you leave, don't give anyone the impression they have just been made. Your name is Bennett, your old name must be forgotten," and, "don't do anything to attract attention to yourselves."

Rebecca and the family drove away from the back of their shop and headed north. David had been over the route they were to take many times in his mind. The first large town was to be Magdeburg.

Travelling through the small towns and villages of northern Germany was pleasant, despite the stress they were under. No one could imagine that the cloak of peacefulness, covered a monster so vile and evil as Hitler.

The trip, so far had been uneventful. Passing through Magdeburg they took the Hamburg road, turning northeast before getting to the city towards Lübek, and then heading north for the direction of Flensburg on the border with Denmark.

They ate some of the food they had brought with them as they drove along, and were making fairly good progress. Most people trying to leave headed west to Switzerland or France.

The Bennetts (Benes) were pretty sure the German Gestapo had watched their home and shop. They heard later that their shop had been looted. They had left just in time.

David Bennett hoped to be in Denmark before stopping for fuel, but as they were getting low David pulled into a petrol station. He asked for petrol using sign language. The owner of the station eventually understood that they wanted the tank of the car filled up. David continued speaking English to the man, but the only response he got was "Ya, Ya". After David and all left, the German thought 'the English are a bit different.' They looked English anyway.

The journey was continued north toward Flensburg, arriving in late evening. They were stopped at the border by German guards. David explained they were English tourists on their way home to England. Uncle David had asked them for photographs of the four of them, and had sent them four passports. David wondered how he had managed to get them, but he never said. The passports looked somewhat used, but were accepted wherever presented. The German guards moved them through the border, and Danish police stopped them at the other side. They presented the passports again, and were waved onto Denmark. The relief was quite evident. They could relax a little but had a long way to go.

Their destination was now Esbjerg, on the west coast of Denmark. When they neared Esbjerg, they by chance heard of a cargo ship, which sailed from there to Harwich on the east coast of England, about a hundred miles from London. They had booked in at a hotel near the docks, and the proprietor, after hearing that their luggage had been stolen in Germany, understood why they had come through to Denmark to get home to England.

The party drove down to the docks and Mr Bennett

enquired about getting a passage home. There always seemed to be someone they met in Denmark who could speak English.

David asked the ship's agent specifically about the ship. He had heard from the hotel proprietor that he was going to Harwich, England, and again the party was in luck. They acquired the passage and soon drove their German-made car down to the ship. David, Ruth, and Rebecca were soon on board and the car fitted in a small space where some of the cargo stood.

They had expected to leave the car behind but agreed they would take it if at all possible. If they had to leave it behind, it would have been a small price to pay for their freedom.

One of the crew said he couldn't understand why they, or why anyone, would take a German car home to England. David heard the remark and told the sailor he had a Jewish friend in Germany who had given it to him. The sailor looked hard at him and all the party, and growled, "Some people get all the luck." – little did he know.

David went then to the telegraph office to send a message to David's uncle that he had hoped to send for some time. The message was, "Arriving Harwich, England, 8 a.m. June 22nd aboard cargo ship *Labit*." David went back to get them all on board.

The Bennett family, plus their English tutor relaxed for the first time, having escaped Germany. Their voyage was uneventful, except that Sarah had been seasick. There were other passengers, some Danish and a few English people. There were also some German people who, they found out later, were also Jews. They kept to themselves, and the Bennetts made no effort to talk with them.

Their first sight of England was a smudge on the horizon, which as they got nearer, gradually grew into land.

Finally they neared the pier and the family, with Rebecca, went to the side of the boat from which they disembarked.

Looking down from the ship they saw small gatherings of people waiting to meet passengers, and to David's delight and relief he saw his uncle among them. Then came the next hurdle to get over. Going through Customs, they were asked if they had anything to declare, and where they were going. Luckily David had his uncle's address which he presented to them, then they were allowed through Customs to be greeted by Uncle David.

After introducing Rebecca to Uncle David, they told him of her part in teaching them English…They had made it.

Their car was unloaded, and then the police stopped them when they reached the dock gates, suspicious of the German car with right-hand drive. David explained again that the car belonged to some German Jews who had sold it to him for a very low price. The police wished them a safe trip home, and off they drove, following Uncle David.

Driving down towards London Uncle David pulled his car into a restaurant parking lot. They all went inside and ate breakfast and Uncle David explained his plan to them…

They were not going back to his home but to a small seaside town on the English Channel coast. There was a small tailor's shop for sale there, and Uncle David explained that he would lend them the money to buy the premises. With it came some stock and furnishings included in the sale price. It would give them a start anyway.

Mr Bennett followed Uncle David who now had Sarah as a passenger.

They arrived in Midhampton, the little town on the south coast, and registered at a hotel.

All the shops were closed and after supper they all walked around the town, down to the wharf and along the pier. They had never seen small fishing-boats before and wondered how such small craft stayed afloat when at sea.

On the way back to the hotel they passed the tailor's shop and the house adjoining. It looked good, and David thought, 'anything was better than what they had left behind in Germany'. They now had the opportunity to buy the shop, and the possibility of peace of mind.

They hadn't seen too much of the town but liked what they saw. Uncle David agreed they would negotiate the purchase the next day.

Luckily on the way back to the hotel, David was able to get some medicine at a chemist shop that was still open, to treat Sarah for her seasickness, which was still bothering her. It happened to be Tom Carter's chemist shop, and Tom found one of his well-proved remedies for stomach upset that always seemed to work. Tom asked if David and his family were on holiday – and immediately David was on guard, then quickly relaxed, remembering they were now in England – not Germany.

They then chattered for a while and David explained that he was interested in the tailor's shop that was for sale a little way down the street. Tom remarked that, "It would be nice to have the shop opened again, and the previous owner had done well there." David explained that he was a tailor by trade. Tom, after thinking for a while, invited David and his family to come to supper that evening if they bought the shop and premises.

The Bennett family went to the Estate Agent in charge of selling the shop, for the owners. After a short wait they were taken to view the property.

Uncle David said, "After the viewing, we will discuss the purchase amongst themselves, and will contact the agent when they have decided one way or another." Uncle

David said that he thought the price was a bit high and the agent assured him the owners were open to an offer.

David told the agent, that if they bought the premises they would want to move it right away. The agent said that he was sure that would be possible.

The Bennett family could hardly contain the excitement. They liked the town, the view of the sea, and really liked the shop and premises.

As the headed toward the front door to leave, Uncle David turned to David and said quietly, "Can you manage to afford 10% less than the asking price?" He said it just loud enough for the agent to hear, David replied that he could see his way clear, bearing in mind the amount of material Uncle David was holding for him.

Uncle David told the estate agent, they had thought in over, and had decided there and then to purchase. An offer was made slightly more that the 10%, and they settled the deal, and the conditions still applied that they could move in straight away.

Rebecca and Sarah had been listening in the background, as Uncle David, David and Ruth did the transaction. By tomorrow they would own a home and business in England.

By now Rebecca was considered to be one of the family, and would stay with the Bennett's until an opportunity came for her to get a job.

Later that day the Bennett family and Rebecca returned to the chemist shop and told Tom they had bought the Tailor's shop and were moving in the next day. The estate agent saw no reason for any delay in quickly completing the deal as the former owner's family had owned the property for generations, no mortgage had to be arranged so the completion date was immediate.

Tom was very pleased they were moving in; he thought they would be an asset to the town, and also, the town needed a tailor.

David told Tom about the cloth in store in Uncle David's warehouse, and that the investment he had made in it whist in Germany, would now be of benefit to them.

Tom reminded them that they had been invited to supper, and they all went along to meet Ellen, Sarah and Rose.

This was the first time Ben was to meet Sarah. After a good supper, whilst grown-ups were talking Ben offered to show Sarah his garden. The roses were in bloom and were beautiful and Sarah was overjoyed when Ben took out his pocketknife and cut the biggest and best rose Sarah had ever seen, and gave it to her. Ben didn't really know why he did that, but it seemed the right thing to do at that moment. Sarah never forgot that large red rose. Ben and Sarah rejoined the families, Sarah showing off her red rose, which also impressed the Bennett's.

David Bennett remarked, "England and roses seem to go together, not like…" He suddenly stopped speaking, he hesitated before he spoke again – and said, "Not like Germany."

David knew one day someone would find out that they were Jews, so he said quietly, not knowing what the consequences would be… "The Bennett family are Jews," expecting to be asked to leave. David and Ruth were surprised to hear Tom say, "I can't see anything wrong with that. We are Church of England and that doesn't in any way bother us," he added. "A lot of people call our vicar 'Hellfire Jack', but that's not his real name of course – of course." There was laughter, everybody relaxed and from that time the two families gradually became great friends.

David explained how the Bennett family had escaped from Germany, and the circumstances leading up to their departure. Ellen said, "I am sure, very sure, nothing like that would ever happen here."

Sarah enrolled in the local school, the same one Ben attended.

Ben didn't like it at all. He was more interested in what was going on in his life. He loved to go down to the harbour and work at the *Syrup of Figs*, as their boat became known. Tom Carter didn't plan to name his boat after a can of mild laxative, but after being in the harbour for a few weeks it became known by that name, as a matter of course.

Ben enjoyed the trips out to the lobster traps. He would re-bait the traps and hope for more lobsters next time out.

Ben disliked one of his schoolteacher's Miss Taylor. Ben described her to his parent as bad tempered and having old teeth, which occasionally showed when she tried to smile, upon rare occasions. She, Miss Taylor, didn't like Ben either, and there was a lot of tension between them. The remaining staff Ben got along with fairly well. Ben saw them as a group of bossy, arrogant people who had taken away his freedom. He was more interested in his garden, in which he worked under the supervision of his grandmother.

By the time he was twelve years old Ben established several customers who purchased from him. By that time, his father allowed Ben out to sea on his own. The first time Sarah went fishing, there was trouble. She had not told her parents she was going out to sea and this resulted in Sarah being banned from ever going out in a boat with Ben again.

Sarah and Ben were always together with Ben's dog, Meg, which he had acquired by accident – it was a stray dog, and had attached itself to Ben. Meg was a Labrador mixture, and very faithful to Ben after a few days. No one claimed her, and no one wanted to own her.

Local people were used to seeing Sarah and Ben

together, which they usually were. They were never far apart, and got along very well.

The Bennetts relented after a few weeks and Sarah and Meg were then usually on board when Ben went to sea. Mr Carter insisted, with authority, that they only went out when the sea was calm, and no wind forecast.

Ben and Sarah became quite expert at catching fish, which Ben sold. Both families, Bennetts and Carters had a good supply of lobster and fish.

Ben and Sarah used to enjoy spending some evenings with Rose. She always seemed to return to the same subject, which was about her days on the farm. Every field seemed to have a story, which was always interesting. They were especially pleased when she spoke of the lake in the woods, in the centre of the farm. She used to tell them about the south Devon cattle, the rich milk they produced and the lovely yellow butter made from the cream that was then sold. Rose also told them about the heavy horses, Clydesdales that used to do the work of ploughing etc.

Ben got on fairly well at school now and he learned quickly, but he still looked upon school as something he didn't care much for. He didn't know why he saved his money; he didn't go short very much. Rose had opened an account for him at the local bank when he was born. She put £5 in his account, which was added to by money he received for his birthdays and Christmas. The bank manager was used to seeing him in the bank. Ben, always polite, would make his deposit and leave.

At the far end of the Carter property was an old barn and a field; the north being part of the property which adjoined the Carter property. One day there appeared an advertisement in the local paper: "Barn and 10 acres of land for sale, £500." Ben saw it and thought hard about the property. Ben's garden was far too small now for him to expand his vegetable production. He told his father that he would really like to purchase the field. Tom responded, "Who would pay for it, boy?" Ben left feeling rejected. Ellen had heard the conversation between Ben and Tom, and told Tom that she had seen Ben's Bank saving book. He had saved over £700, and he had earned most of it himself, and should be able to spend it himself on such a project as purchasing property.

Ellen said, "The money will be just as safe being invested in a field with a barn, as it will be in a bank."

Tom told Ellen that Ben would have to be 21 years old before he could buy property. Tom said, "I'll ask Rose what she thinks about it. She often has words of wisdom."

Ben asked Rose before Tom got a chance to. He explained to his grandmother what he wanted to do i.e. purchase the adjoining field. Again, the question come up, by Rose this time. "How will you pay for it?" Ben produced his savings book, showing over £700. The astonished look on Rose's face said it all. She made the same remark that Ellen had said. "You have saved the money, without being told to, and should be able to spend it." Rose approved of the project.

Tom and Ellen went to see Rose. They explained what Ben wanted to do. Rose said, "I know – Ben told me this morning, and I told him I thought it was a good idea." Tom again pointed out that Ben had to be of age to purchase property, to which the old lady replied with some sadness, "My Charlie bought his first field before he was 21. If you like I will see the solicitor, and I will offer Ben the opportunity to put the property in my name. I will ask the solicitor to put it in his fancy words – to make sure Ben is in fact the owner. This is what my Charlie did. There is one other thing – let Ben do as much towards the transaction as he would like to."

Tom broke the news to Ben when he came home from seeing his lobster traps. Sarah was with Ben, as she always seemed to be. They were both delighted.

Ben asked his father, "What do I do now?" To which Tom replied that bearing in mind his mother-in-law's advise, "you will have to go to the Estate Agent and ask about it. Then, if he is agreeable, make him an offer, a bit less than the asking price of £500, say £475 and see what his reaction is."

Ben and Sarah skipped school the following day, and went to see the estate agent. Mr Gregory, the agent, was at the front desk in the office. Ben explained that he was there to purchase the property advertised in the paper, a ten-acre field with barn. Mr Gregory's response was bewilderment. He had never had such a young potential buyer. He asked Ben and Sarah if they were serious and he further asked: "Does your father know about your wanting to buy the field, and what about your grandmother. Does she approve?"

After a little thought Gregory said, "So you will pay £500 for the field? Ben said "No, I have £450 in the bank, and that will be my offer for the field."

Mr Gregory looked at them long and hard, a look that Ben and Sarah never forgot. "You now own a field." They were pleased. They both signed an agreement to purchase. Later in the day Rose went with Ben to see the solicitor, and explained to him what had transpired. Ben asked Sarah to be there, and when Mr Lawton asked whose names would be on the conveyance, Ben said, "My grandmother of course, my name, and Sarah Bennett."

"She has helped me for no reward for some time and she should own part of the field."

Mr Lawton was quite astonished. Rose turned to the window to try to hide the tears that were running down her face, and remarked, "Just like my Charlie."

Later in the week Mr Bennett and Mr Carter went to the solicitor's office at Ben and Sarah's request to witness their signatures on the deed, with Rose signing too. At the west side of the property there was a large fir tree growing in the hedge, this tree was visible from the sea, and it was one of Ben's landmarks when the fog came in low over the sea.

Ben could see the top of the tree above the fog, and line it up with the farmhouse a way beyond. The other landmark was the church steeple, and another farmhouse beyond. When he could see all four in line then he was over the area of his lobster traps at sea.

In Germany, Hitler was now rounding up the Jewish people, stealing their property and possessions, and herding them off to concentration camps.

The Bennett family were into their business and very relieved to have left Germany when they did.

Sarah especially was far happier in England, than she ever was in Germany. David's business prospered with the help of his wife Ruth. The shop was always busy with customers.

Rebecca helped in the shop until she managed to get a job as a translator working for the Red Cross. She was ideally suited for the job, and she had a good disposition.

The years prior to 1939 were peaceful years; no one who had experienced the horror and devastation of the 1914-1918 war could believe that another was imminent.

In September 1939 the weather was excellent, sunny and warm. Despite warnings from Winston Churchill, no one expected a war to break out. The Germans invaded Poland. Mr Chamberlain, the British Prime Minister, gave the German Government until September 3rd to withdraw from Poland, by 11 a.m.

The Carter family and Sarah Bennett drove west along the coast. They fully expected the Germans would withdraw from Poland. They arrived in the seaside town of Weymouth in the late morning, and were on a paddle steamer for a trip out to sea. Ben had never been on any boat much larger than the *Syrup of Figs*. They had looked forward to an enjoyable trip, and all was going well until they were a few miles offshore, when they heard over the ship's radio that Mr Chamberlain had declared war on behalf of the British Government against Germany. All went quiet onboard. People were very sad at the prospect of another war. The paddle wheeler was turned round and headed back to Weymouth.

Ben took a look at the old paddle wheeler, never expecting to see her again. The Carters and Sarah headed for home, the weather had changed from a sunny day to a cloudy afternoon with light rain; they arrived home in the early evening and Sarah was driven to her home. David and Ruth greeted her with relief. David took Tom Carter aside and asked, now that war had been declared against Germany, "Would that mean we will be arrested and deported. Technically we are Germans."

Tom assured David that this would not happen though, deep down, he wasn't really sure.

When Tom, Ellen and Ben arrived home, Tom telephoned his Member of Parliament, and was lucky to be able to speak to him. The problem of the Bennett family was carefully explained by Tom. The M.P. promised to see that the Bennett family were treated as refugees, and would send application forms for the Bennett's to apply for British citizenship.

Tom walked the short distance to the Bennett's shop, he knocked on the front door but the Bennett's had gone to bed early. Tom Carter knocked on the door again, harder this time – this caused panic in the Bennett family. They thought the authorities had come to arrest them. They were Germans, as Mr Bennett had explained, and also Jewish. It took Tom quite a while to calm them, once they had opened the door, and realized who it was. Tom then explained to them how he had been in touch with their Member of Parliament, and hopefully they would soon be British subjects, and being Jews made no difference.

Tom enquired whether they had been issued with gas masks. Everyone had to have one by law.

They sorted through the cardboard boxes in their back room and finally found the masks, They never expected to use them, how wrong they were.

The German armed forces, despite strong resistance from the Polish people, soon conquered the western part of Poland. The Russians had made a prior agreement with the Germans on how to partition Poland between Polish people, despite a pact made with them to help if they were attacked. Many Polish military did escape, and eventually found their way to Britain.

In England children were evacuated from the cities to the country, leaving behind parents and family, for the safety of less populated areas. A whole school was evacuated to Ben's town, the majority were placed in good homes, but some were not so lucky. They settled in the little town and villages surrounding, some stayed after the war was over.

News came of the sinking of one of Britain's biggest battleships *The Royal Oak*. A U-Boat had entered Scapa-flow, which was supposed to be a safe anchorage for the home fleet. Several more ships were quickly sunk by German U-Boats elsewhere. The good news came when the Royal Navy destroyers *Ajax, Achillies* and *Exeter* caused the sinking of the German battleship *Graf-Spee*. Other than the sinking of ships not much else seemed to happen at that time.

The British expeditionary force was sent to France, expecting the Germans to attack any time. Then all that was heard was, "All's quiet on the western front." No bombing, no expected gas attack, some of the evacuees went back to their homes in London.

Ben and Sarah went out in the *Syrup of Figs* to attend the lobster traps. Everything seemed unreal. There was not any effort on either side to make war. The British Empire and Commonwealth Empire were supporting the motherland as best they could. Canadians, Australians, New Zealanders and South Africans began arriving in Britain. Mr Bennett began to realize and understand what the British Empire stood for.

In late spring, 1940, the Germans attacked Norway. The British sent help but were unable to stem the German tide.

Denmark fell to the Germans and then Holland was invaded, and surrendered after a few days. The Germans attacked Belgium, through which France was attacked. The German armies broke through the French and reached the Channel ports of Calais and Boulogne.

The Belgian king sympathised with the Germans and ordered his army to surrender. The British army was now surrounded with its back to the sea on Dunkirk. There is not an army in the world that can fight a rear-guard action, but they fought as none other, holding the Germans as the British retreated, back toward Dunkirk. The situation was desperate.

The order was given to evacuate the army by sea, but how? There were not enough ships, and there was hope by the Government that perhaps 25,000 men could be rescued. King George VI, on the following Sunday, called for a National Day of Prayer. All who could go to Church should pray for the army and for help for the desperate situation Britain was in. Mr Bennett went to see Tom Carter, and asked his advice about what to do. He was told to attend Church if he could, most others would go, and if he didn't go, under the circumstances, it would not look right.

Mr Bennett replied, "There is no synagogue locally." Tom countered this by saying, "Then you must go to the Church of England, you don't have to become a Christian, or do anything to compromise your religion, just go to the church and do the same as everyone else. There will be people in the congregation who haven't been to church for years, and they will have forgotten the ritual of the service, so you will be the same as they will be."

David Bennett thought aloud, 'Will it do any good?' A quick sharp reply from Tom said, "Your people did all right when the walls of Jericho came down."

On Sunday the church was packed with people, as was expected. Many generations had prayed, especially in times of need. David had told his wife they were going to church on the morrow. Ruth refused at first – David explained how kind the English had been to them, and they would all go. One hymn stayed in David's mind. They all sang, "Oh God our Help in ages past, our hope for years to come." They were all praying to God.

Admiral Ramsey, of the Royal Navy was at his wits end as to how he could bring home the British forces trapped at Dunkirk. He asked over the BBC for anyone who owned a boat to help to bring home the British expeditionary force. He was not expecting too much response.

The British Government expected 25,000 might be transported home, and even that figure they thought was high.

The following day Admiral Ramsey was taken to the coast. From a cliff top he looked out over the eastern English Channel. There were boats as far as he could see, boats of every size and description, all heading east.

From the east coast of England another armada of boats was putting out to sea. From the Thames estuary everything that would float was sailing, one common purpose, and one destination: Dunkirk.

Admiral Ramsey and his staff were witnessing the impossible.

After hearing Admiral Ramsey's broadcast on the BBC, Tom Carter and five local fishermen decided they would all go to Dunkirk.

There were the Gibson's, known as Harry, Walter Tuck, Dick Bugler, Jim Jessom, Bill Watson, and Henry Ball. They decided they would all go.

Looking out to sea boats were already passing by, up the English Channel. Provisions were put on the boats. Seldom had any of them sailed more than three miles from the harbour, as some had never heard of Dunkirk, let alone knew how far away it was, or where it was.

An army truck came down to the wharf loaded with petrol, cans (two gallons capacity) square, and easy to stack. They were packed on the seven boats. Tom Carter took twenty cans on board, tied together side-by-side in the front of the boat. He packed forty-eight tins of corned beef in one locker, and in the other he put twenty-four bottles of beer. This was all stored in the front section of the boat. Ben helped to get things together, and fully expected to go with his father. Tom refused to let him go. He told Ben he didn't know what was in store for any of them, and asked him to stay, and look after his mother and family. Sarah had been standing by, and heard the conversation, and was very relieved Ben was not going.

Harry Gibson left first; he hugged his wife who had helped him get his boat ready. Harry started the engine, and slowly pulled away from the harbour. He increased speed and headed east.

The next boat to leave was Walter Tuck's. A small man was Walter, with a heart bigger than most. He and his wife were always rowing and arguing in public or anywhere else they might be. Despite this they got on well really. Today was no exception, a first-class row broke out when Walter was about to leave. Jessie, his wife, said she would never speak to Walter again, quickly followed by wishing Walter a safe trip.

Ellen Cater managed the shop, and couldn't get away to get down to the wharf. When Tom had everything ready on board he went home to say goodbye. He was in a hurry to get back to the *Syrup of Fig*, when he tripped over a piece of rope, and broke his ankle. He was taken to the local hospital, where the bone was set, and the lower part of his leg put in a cast. There would be no way he could go to Dunkirk.

The other boats left as soon as they were ready to go. They planned to sail together. The most powerful of the five remaining boats pulled ahead and left the others. Dick Bugler's boat parted from the others the following night. There were boats everywhere. Dick found in the early morning that the two boats along side him were from another harbour – the other boats lost contact with each other when they arrived at Dunkirk. They had all planned to sail together, now they were on their own.

Ben and Sarah visited the hospital to see Tom. He was in pain, but told the nursing staff and his doctor, who lived near his shop, that he had to get home to the chemist shop, as there was no one there capable or skilled enough to make up the prescriptions. Ben wondered who would have seen to the prescriptions if his father had gone to Dunkirk. A wheelchair was found for Tom in the hospital, and at home a bed was brought down from upstairs to the living room. He could then be wheeled to the counter to make up the prescriptions.

Tom had done what he thought was necessary, putting supplies in the boat. He, like most others who took their boats, didn't know what they were all in for.

Ben and Sarah walked down to the wharf. The *Syrup*

of Figs was the only boat left. The boat rose and fell as the small waves in the harbour influenced the motion.

When Ben and Sarah arrived at the wharf Meg the dog, their faithful friend, was with them. Even she looked forlorn at the empty harbour. She was used to going out in the boat fishing with them but today they didn't go. Meg always ran free and was very seldom on a leash.

Ben and Sarah discussed the boats that had left for Dunkirk, wondering how the men who sailed them were faring. Boats were still sailing up the English Channel, the smaller boats keeping fairly close to shore, the larger ones further out to sea.

Ben suddenly had an idea. "Why shouldn't he take the *Syrup of Figs* to Dunkirk." He felt he could handle the boat as well as his father. In fact, lately he used the boat more than his father. The boat was ready to go with petrol and supplies on board.

Ben explained the plan to Sarah. She was filled with horror, and they had the worse argument they had ever had. Ben took Meg's leash from his pocket and placed it on Meg's collar and handed it to Sarah. He was going to go. Ben went down the ladder to the boat, Meg trying to follow, as she was used to doing. Sarah kept Meg at her side, and tried to calm her down. Sarah was pretty sure that Ben would relent and change his mind and get back up on the pier. She thought she had cried all her tears when Ben untied the *Syrup of Figs* and started the engine. Another bout of crying started, part anger and part frustration. She could only watch, as he coaxed more speed from the engine.

The Norton 500cc engine was noisy, powerful and very reliable but not made for a boat, especially for a long, non-stop journey.

There was a point of land jutting out into the sea, there were rocks at the end of the land, and boats gave it a wide berth. Sarah expected Ben to turn the boat around and come home. He didn't, he turned and briefly waved and disappeared around the 'point', as it was commonly known.

Sarah still waited, hoping he would reappear. The silence at the harbour was unusual. Normally someone would be working at something on the boats. Even in foul weather someone would be around, tending ropes to keep the boats from damage etc. Like many harbours, south, east, and west of England, the harbours were empty of boats, ships, and anything that would float.

Sarah walked slowly to the Carter house with Meg showing her bewilderment, somehow knowing things were not right. Sarah walked onto the Carter's shop. Mr Carter was making up prescriptions for his customers and Ellen was working at something behind the counter. She looked up from what see was doing. Sarah started to cry again, she knew she had to tell them about Ben. Seeing Sarah's tears, Tom immediately thought Ben was in trouble. Ben and Sarah were always together, that was how they were. They had been together since Sarah arrived from Germany.

Sarah blurted between her sobs, "Ben has gone." Ellen asked, "Where has Ben gone Sarah?"

"He's gone to Dunkirk." Sarah replied. The Carters tried to console Sarah, telling her that Ben would soon come back, when he was out to sea, away from home, and having thought over what he was doing.

After a while Sarah walked back to the harbour, no sign of Ben, just an unusually quiet harbour. Ben had gone, and so had everyone else who had a boat. Sarah walked to her home. She told her parents Ben had gone, and to where he was going. They could not hide their concern and astonishment.

Ruth Bennett said, "But he is only 13 years old." Mr Bennett countered, "He can handle that boat better then anyone else." He was sure, he said, that Ben would be back. Deep down David Bennett had a gut feeling that if there were a way to get to Dunkirk, Ben would find it.

The Bennett's walked out of their shop to look to sea. There were still boats passing going east. The boats from the Southwest of England were joining in the efforts to bring the British army home that was trapped at Dunkirk.

Ben sat in the rear of the boat, the *Syrup of Figs*. He managed to steer with his right arm over the tiller, and he found the engine was too powerful for the boat, so kept it at half-throttle to prevent the boat from bucking. He found the boat would ride one wave and hit the next, pushing the bow deep into the water when trying to do anything faster.

Most of the boats were making better headway than Ben was. There were three boats, Ben remembered, all painted the same colour, and of the same design. He could see two men on each boat.

Their boats had twin propellers, making them capable of much more speed than Ben was able to make. Painted on the front of the boats, Ben made out the numbers and the port they were from: Brixham. They had travelled 150 miles, at least, Ben worked out, one following the other. After a while the front boat changed places with the rear one. Ben realized they were working in the wake of one another. Far behind him, Ben noticed something on the horizon; a smudge of smoke, and then a larger boat eventually appeared.

This boat too, was faster than the *Syrup of Figs*. Ben couldn't make out what kind of ship would make such a smoke. After an hour or so Ben could make out foam being churned up on the ship's side exposed to his view. Then he realized it was the paddle wheeler from Weymouth, driven by an old steam engine. Ben remembered seeing the engine, when his father had taken him down below, when they made their trip to Weymouth. The captain was one of the few who had some idea about the distance to Dunkirk. He knew they would need the maximum amount of coal to travel the distance of the round trip. It never entered his head that he may not come back.

Then came the wait for steam. Getting steam up took time. The fire was lit in the engine, and coal added, which eventually gave a tremendous heat. Wind was blown into the firebox with a fan to increase the coal consumption and thus produce more heat, which in turn gave more steam and power.

There were four men on the paddle steamer besides the two stokers. The stokers took turns in shovelling coal into the furnace, letting water into the engine every half hour to make steam to drive the engine, which drove the two big wheels either side of the boat.

The paddle wheeler was now working at full-steam ahead.

The captain stayed in the wheelhouse steering what he called his 'pride and joy.' He had served in the Royal Navy, and was wondering what would happen when and if he reached Dunkirk.

Ben watched the paddle steamer gradually approach the *Syrup of Figs*. There was another boat Ben had not noticed before, the paddle steamer having taken most of his attention. Then his interest turned to the newcomer.

There were two men in this one. Ben estimated the boat to be at least twenty-feet long, driven by two propellers. He couldn't make out the name, but she was registered in Penzance, Cornwall. The boat had already travelled more than two hundred miles. To Ben's surprise the Penzance boat slowed speed and came over to the *Syrup of Figs*. The two men on board expressed their concern for Ben's boat, being so far out in the Channel. Ben explained he could not get any more speed, and told them why. Both boats, the Penzance, and the *Syrup of Figs* were moving slowly side-by-side. The men on board told Ben to get in behind the paddleboat, about 150 yards behind, between the waves of the wake of the large ship.

Before the men pulled ahead they asked Ben where he was from, and said they would not have enough fuel and was any available in Midhampton. Ben said he was sure there would be. The Cornish boat was running on diesel fuel. There were several farm tractors that used diesel in the area around Midhampton. So there should be some available. The men on the Penzance boat were more than surprised to see a boy sailing a boat on such a terrible errand. They wished Ben good luck and accelerated away leaving the *Syrup of Figs*.

Ben then turned his attention to the paddle wheeler. Taking the advice of the Cornishmen, he eased the *Syrup of Figs* closer to the paddle wheeler. He waited for the opportunity to cross the wave made by the ship. He was then about the distance the Cornishmen had suggested. All he had to do was swing the boat at right angles made by the bigger boat. Ben waited for the opportune moment, pulled the tiller over, met the wave head-on and was now meeting the smaller swells.

Ben turned the *Syrup of Figs* to travel behind the paddle wheeler. The Cornishmen were right, the sea was calmer. Ben was able to increase speed, and was able to keep up with the larger boat.

Ben had been worried about finding the way to Dunkirk, now all he had to do was follow along behind the paddle wheeler. He felt more secure than at any time so far on the journey.

Ben secured the tiller whilst he refuelled the engine. He hadn't eaten for several hours. He took a tin of corned beef from the box stashed in the front of the boat, drew some water from the drum beside the corned beef stash and found a packet of biscuits his father had put in. He returned to his seat suddenly realizing how hungry he was. He enjoyed his meal.

The exhaust from the Norton 500cc passed under removable planks in the bottom of the boat. Ben took one of the planks off, and immediately felt the warmth from the exhaust. He pulled part of the tarpaulin over his knees and over the heated area made by the exhaust. Ben settled down in this spot in the back of the boat. He released the tiller, which he kept under his right arm, and relaxed, still following behind the paddle wheeler. Ben had never enjoyed a meal more than this one. He was less anxious about the situation he had got himself into.

The sun was setting behind him. The cliffs, usually white, were now pink in colour from the setting sun. The night was going to be a long one.

At regular intervals the stokers in the paddle wheeler were putting on more coal causing smoke, for a while, to billow from the single stack of the ship. Some sparks would show from the fire down below in the darkness of the coming night. Ben was thankful that the boat was showing him the way. He felt gratitude for the Cornishmen's advice.

Ben's grandmother Rose had an old gramophone. She played the old machine quite often, enjoying records of Gilbert and Sullivan. Ben especially remembered the "Pirates of Penzance". If the two men he had seen were pirates, they were certainly very helpful ones.

The darkness of night was fast approaching. They were now amongst more boats all heading east; boats from every port along the Channel coast. Big boats, small boats, Ben never knew Englishmen owned so many.

The captain of the paddle steamer was of the same mind. He walked around the ship, as he called it, then he noticed the small boat behind him. Before darkness fell, he looked at the boat through his binoculars. He could see quite plainly the sole occupant was only a boy. The captain waved, and Ben returned the wave. The captain returned to his cabin, and remarked to the men who were steering, "Did you see that small boat fairly close behind?" To which they replied, "Yes!"

The captain said, "Did you see the young fellow sailing her?"

"Yes," was the reply. "I don't think he will come to any harm where he is – I don't think he can be more than 12 or 13 years old. We'll keep an eye on him, but I can't think of anything we can do to help him." The captain thought for a while.

"We have on board somewhere a light. It doesn't give off much light but it may serve the purpose of giving him something to follow in the darkness," the captain said. Adding, "I'll tie it to the back of the ship. I'll make it so that no one can see it, except from behind."

It was really dark by now and Ben was getting extremely tired. He dozed for a few minutes, not long enough to dream, but woke up abruptly and then doze again. To Ben's relief he saw the light the captain had tied to the back of the paddle steamer. Ben then settled down for the night, he kept warm from the engine exhaust, and thought he had things under control. The night seemed long and never ending. The paddle steamer changed course slightly to the southeast. Ben followed and soon saw the reason. There were boats returning from Dunkirk east of them in order to prevent collisions with the boats going out to Dunkirk.

Several of the returning boats were packed with soldiers, some with so much weight they sailed low in the water. For the first time Ben asked himself, "How many could the *Syrup of Figs* get on board?" He thought the extreme limit would be ten, five on each side. He didn't worry too much; they hadn't got near a beach yet. Further east Royal Navy ships were moving very fast. As the dawn broke Ben could make out hundreds of boats, some on their way to Dunkirk, and others on their way home.

As darkness had completely lifted Ben heard the first gunfire and saw the flashes of guns. The German planes were attacking the large ships. The navy was returning the fire. Ben had never seen or heard anything like it. Not in his wildest imagination could he have anticipated the situation he was in now. Ben was very frightened to say the least. A German fighter plane came in very low, and machine-gunned the paddle steamer. No damage seemed to have been done. The old paddle steamer kept up her speed. Ben tagged along behind with the throttle three-quarters open, as it had been from the time he had got behind the bigger ship.

Things were quiet for a while. The next attack took place mid-morning and no one could have prepared Ben or any of the others sailing their boats, for the horror that was taking place. The planes were again after the larger ships and the Royal Navy was doing all it could manage.

The paddle steamer was attacked a second time. The noise was awful. Bombs were being dropped as well as machine guns firing. Ben could see the crosses on the planes and knew they were Germans.

The attack was at its height when from the direction of England Ben could see planes flying very low and coming straight towards him. He didn't know whose planes they were, and assumed they were German. He went forward from his seat in the back of the boat onto the bottom of the *Syrup of Figs*. They turned out to be British planes; he didn't know whether they were Spitfires or Hurricanes. They came up under the German planes which were bombing the ships. It was the first time Ben had ever seen a plane shot down. Two German planes went down from the RAF attack. Ben had never even been close to a plane before, he resumed his seat after the attack, and took up the tiller and pressed on. Ben knew now he couldn't return. It would be just as dangerous to turn as to stay on course. Ben didn't realise how close they were getting to landing. The captain of the paddle steamer now wondered what do to about the small boat behind, which had kept up with his boat across the English Channel. He decided to go to the back of the paddle steamer, and try to think of a way to divert the small boat away to the west, which would take Ben's boat straight to the beaches of Dunkirk.

The Captain waved his arms above his head, from side-to-side, and then pointed to the west. Ben, at first, didn't understand, but then realised the significance of the captain's gestures. Ben slowed his speed, eased the boat over the wave forming from the west side of the paddle steamer, and headed straight for a beach.

Ben now experienced shelling from German artillery, which increased as he got nearer to the beach. The Germans were bombing the beaches. Luckily because of the material the beaches were made of, the sand allowed the German bombs to go deep before exploding. Ben estimated he was about one mile off shore as the low cliffs of the French coast were plainly visible. German aircraft were bombing and machine-gunning the soldiers. Again the bombs continued to go deep in the sand and exploding causing less casualties than if they had exploded on first impact.

The German artillery grew more intense as more of their guns were brought into battle; German fighters machine-gunned the boats and beaches; it was Hell on Earth.

A small company of British soldiers was trying to hold their final position. Sergeant Dawson was in charge. The company used to be forty strong with two officers. Ten days previously they had been advancing from France into Belgium, bewildered by the change, from advancing into Belgium. They steadily retreated to partly prepare positions, which they held for a while, until the Germans forced them back again. They had suffered their first casualties, but luckily no one was killed. The wounded were evacuated and eventually put upon hospital ships bound for England. There were a few hours lull in the fighting. None of the men had ever been in action before. They had been trained but that was no preparation for what was now taking place.

Another German attack, more casualties, eventually withdrawing, they had been fighting now for over a week; they were part of a rear-guard, trying to hold the Germans at bay to enable the army to evacuate as many soldiers as possible. The small company, eleven men out of forty, crouched in their last position before the beach to the west of Dunkirk. They could see boats taking off from the shore a bit to their east. Sergeant Dawson spoke to the survivors of the company. He explained to the company what they already knew i.e. they were out of ammunition, and had no food or water. They would have to try to get on a boat or surrender. Dawson realised there was no point in going to the beach. There were too many soldiers ahead on the beach, and they would be easy targets for the Germans.

"We are fairly safe here," he said. "The basement and rubble of the demolished house gave them some protection. "If the Germans attack, we have nothing to protect ourselves with and will have to surrender and have to become prisoners of war. We have done our best," he said. They hunted through the rubble for anything to eat, but found absolutely nothing. The water pipes were empty. The rifles were of no use as they had run out of ammunition. Sergeant Dawson knew their plight was desperate and was himself resigned to becoming a prisoner of war at best.

In late afternoon Sergeant Dawson was watching the sea. Some of his men slept a little, two of the men watched Sergeant Dawson. Instead of moving the binoculars he was using from side-to-side, he was concentrating on one spot at sea. Sergeant Dawson couldn't believe what he was seeing. Two boats were coming toward the beach; Sergeant Dawson immediately gave orders to his men. "Leave everything behind. We will head down to the beach with as much speed as we can, just in case those two boats I see are coming into shore here."

They starting running as ordered and, to their horror, a German shell hit one of the boats and blew it to pieces. No one could have survived. The other boat stopped, when another shell hit the water where the boat would have been, had it not stopped.

Ben felt sick; he was in that second boat. Before the boat was hit Ben had been talking to the man who sailed her beside the *Syrup of Figs*. They had decided to sail in together and pick up a load of soldiers, and leave as quickly as possibly when then boat was hit. Ben stopped the *Syrup of Figs* wanting to help. Another shell hit the water just in front of him. Ben's terror grew, but he couldn't wait in that spot. It would be his turn next. He started up the engine and went full speed for the shore, bucking the waves it didn't matter, it had to, another shell exploded behind him in the water. Ben turned the *Syrup of Figs* aiming straight for the beach. Soldiers were running towards him as soon as he touched shore. He had to keep the back of the boat out toward the sea to prevent any damage to the propeller hitting the shore. He couldn't start the engine without that risk.

Sergeant Dawson asked Ben how many soldiers he could take on board. Ben replied, "Five men each side of the boat." The British officer came running along the shore. He helped the men get on board and told the sergeant he had somehow become separated from his battalion. They had been ordered down to the port to embark, the Germans had attacked and he somehow got separated from the rest. They must hurry along and try to find his battalion or what was left of them. This left Sergeant Dawson alone on the beach. Ben gave the officer a small card he had written with his father's home address and 'phone number, and said, "If you get home before I do, will you please 'phone him and tell him I am all right." The officer wondered how anybody could be 'alright' in the position Ben was in.

Sergeant Dawson and Ben pushed the *Syrup of Figs* back into the sea. Ben was ready to jump aboard when he suddenly realised Sergeant Dawson was being left behind. Ben, without much thought, said to him, "One more." The boat was already low in the water. Ben placed him in the back of the boat, beside where he usually sat.

The engine of the *Syrup of Figs* started. Ben opened the throttle and slowly the heavily laden boat left the shore of France. Ben could only make low speed, any big wave would have swamped the boat. A German plane machined-gunned the boat; one bullet hit the *Syrup of Figs'* fuel tank, but didn't penetrate the metal. Ben was hit in the forehead by a splinter from the boat, but no one was hurt seriously.

The German plane circled for another attack, when, out of the blue, a British fighter shot the German plane down into the ocean. The German pilot got out of his sinking plane and waved for help. Ben couldn't offer any help, even if he had wanted to, he had too many men on board, and one more could have made it disastrous.

Sergeant Dawson pulled from his pocket, or from somewhere, a bandage and bound up the wound on Ben's head.

Ben increased the speed of the boat slowly, they were

now several hundred yards off shore. The Norton 500cc engine was making more noise with the extra weight on the boat. But like a horse going home from a day's hard work, it seemed a bit faster. To Ben every yard counted, another yard nearer home.

After a while, Sergeant Dawson asked Ben how old he was and was totally amazed that the boy would be where he was on the sea. Ben said, "I am thirteen and will soon be fourteen."

Sergeant Dawson said, "You are very brave, and thank you!" They all said, 'thank you.' And they all meant it. Sergeant Dawson asked Ben if there was anything to drink on board, none expecting there to be. The men were all desperately thirsty. Ben handed the tiller to the Sergeant and went forward to the front of the boat. He opened the small door on the left-hand side, and eased out the five-gallon drum of water. Various things were used to drink from. The company drank their first liquid for more than two days. The drum almost empty, Ben realised there had to be enough left for his own use, and said so. All drinking from the drum immediately ceased.

Ben took the drum and placed it back in the compartment. He then opened the right compartment and to the company's surprise and delight handed everyone a pint of beer. Some sort of a cheer came forth. Ben then reached back into the compartment, and pulled out twelve tins of corned beef that his father had placed in the boat when he was making ready for the trip. All on board cheered again. They couldn't believe what they were seeing. They hadn't eaten for many days. They were familiar with the key on the top of the can, which when clipped on the side of the tin and turned, would cleanly open the can and expose the contents. Ben too had one of the cans. He didn't realize how hungry he had become with all the mayhem and terror he had endured.

Ben then put more petrol in the engine of the *Syrup of Figs*, and all on board settled down for the long trip home.

As Ben stuffed bits of rag in the holes the bullets had made, he wondered what his father's reaction would be. The sea was slightly choppy, not enough to come over the sides of the boat, but enough to prevent them from going any faster.

Several of the soldiers quickly dropped off to sleep, and soon the rest followed. It was their first uninterrupted sleep for over a week.

As Sergeant Dawson had remarked to them earlier, 'they had done their best.'

If the rear guards had given away and the Germans had broken through their defences, there would have been no evacuation from Dunkirk.

The last sunset Ben had seen was on his way over, when he was tagging along behind the paddle steamer. Ben wondered what had become of her.

There were many boats as far as Ben could see, in either direction, all filled with soldiers. All of them seemed to be making better headway and faster than the *Syrup of Figs*. The company on board, when they had woken from their sleep, were interested in the name of the boat, the *Syrup of Figs*. Ben explained, retracing the story of how the fuel tank got to be there. One soldier remarked, "We are bound to get home, running on *Syrup of Figs*.

It was a long night but, for the most part, a starry night. Ben wished he had learned to navigate. He looked back toward France. There was a glow of fire reflected in the sky from Dunkirk. He kept travelling north west from the fires that glowed there at the port of Dunkirk.

The speed of the *Syrup of Figs* was held in check by the weight of the soldiers on board. Had the wind blown they would not have made it thus far. The first light of dawn came none too soon.

Ben could make out other boats around him. Two were quite close. People on board waved, at least he thought 'if the worst happened someone might rescue them.' He could see a problem with that: they were weighed down in the water like the *Syrup of Figs* was.

By daylight Ben could just about make out land. The sun began to appear, showing the way for them. Ben had spread out the tarpaulin, which was normally used to cover the boat when anchored. He placed the tarpaulin over the knees of the soldiers and himself. He removed the two planks over the Norton 500cc engine, which gave them some warmth and some protection from the water, which occasionally came in over the side. How thankful Ben was of his father's idea to raise the sides of the boat by a foot.

The sun gradually gave more warmth. The coast of England slowly became more evident, as the *Syrup of Figs* plodded on so slowly.

Ben went to the front of the boat and fetched another tin of corned beef for each of them plus another bottle of beer each. Ben was not used to drinking beer. His father would give him a small glass, when he drank occasionally. Ben felt the warming effect of the beer, and began to relax, for the first time since leaving home.

Ben told Sergeant Dawson that they would have to keep away from any larger boats because a wake, from even a small boat could swamp them.

Ben eased the throttle, steered the boat slightly west, and headed for the coast. He had some idea where he was but, not being sure, decided they would land anywhere they could – if they made it that far. The petrol was holding out. Ben figured he would have enough petrol to get home, which would save him from going into a bigger harbour.

They put another mile behind them – the coast seemed closer, but not much. Ben was anxiously watching where the other boats were heading. He decided to steer further west by a little. He could see bigger ships in the distance east of him. At that stage of the journey he was taking no chances and there was no room for mistakes. They were now about two miles off shore. There was only a slight wind but even that made the waves bigger.

All on board were getting anxious. Ben cut down the motor a little more. He wasn't taking any chances. Now they were heading straight for the shore.

Ben aimed for a place where the cliff seemed to give way to the shore on either side, down to where the low cliff joined the shore. They were half a mile off-shore. Ben could see people on the shore, they must have spotted Ben's boat heading their way, and so far no rowing boats had landed there. Most, if not all other boats, landing east of them. Ben could see a road heading inland. As the *Syrup of Figs* got closer to shore the waves were getting longer, yet not too much water was coming into the boat. Slowly, Ben eased the *Syrup of Figs* toward the shore. He told the soldier in the front of the boat to throw the rope, which normally tied the boat to the wharf, to anyone who could catch it, in the crowd, which was assembling.

Ben hoped someone would catch the rope, and pulled the boat in straight after the engine was stopped.

The best sound Ben ever heard was when the boat struck the gravel on the beach.

The soldier up front then threw the rope, which was caught by eager hands, and then Sergeant Dawson took over.

He told his men to leave in an orderly way. As they disembarked, the *Syrup of Figs* rose out of the water and as the men left, they were able to pull the boat further up the beach.

They were all given a welcome they would never forget. Someone in the crowd asked, "Where do you pick up the boy?"

The Sergeant replied, "'The boy,' as you call him, owns the boat, and it is he who came over and fetched us, none so brave as he." Ben told them he had to leave soon in order to get home that day. He asked for food and for something to drink, and within half an hour the *Syrup of Figs* was turned around and put back in the water, with the propeller free of the beach. Ben said 'goodbye' to the soldiers and Sergeant Dawson, they thanked him over again, and he was pushed out into the waves.

Ben started up the faithful Norton 500cc and headed west. Ben was homeward bound. Tom Carter was watching from the window of their house overlooking the sea. The boats were sailing west. He wondered if Ben would soon be home, indeed if he was going to make it.

The previous evening Sarah, Tom, Ellen and Rose were sitting listening to the BBC when the phone rung and Tom answered, his wheelchair placed by the phone, where he was seated.

It was the officer that Ben had seen briefly at Dunkirk. He had caught up with his battalion and come home on a navy ship, found the card Ben had given him and telephoned, as he had promised. Tom became very tense.

"So you have seen Ben?" The Officer had replied he had. Tom asked, "Where did you see him?" There was a pause.

"On the beach at Dunkirk."

Horrified Tom asked him, "How was Ben?" The officer explained that Ben had been loading soldiers onto his boat.

Tom asked, "How many?" Then the Officer replied, "At least – ten." Tom responded, "He'll never make it home with that load on board." Tom then asked, "Did you see the boy leave the beach?" The Officer replied in the affirmative, "I know he left, because just off shore a

German fighter plane machined-gunned the boat, the fighter was shot down by a British fighter into the sea. Your son's boat kept going, so I presume no one was hurt badly. The last I saw of him he was about three-hundred yards off-shore. If I should hear more I will be in touch with you." The officer knew the chances of the boat reaching England with that amount of men aboard were very slim.

Tom repeated the phone conversation to the family. "Ben had got to Dunkirk, picked up a group of soldiers and was on his way back. How far would he get? Heaven only knew."

Tom said nothing to them about the *Syrup of Figs* being machine-gunned by a German plane.

Several people were on the wharf at Midhampton, hoping one of the boats would appear.

Boats had been passing by. Out to sea, travelling west, they were hoping soon that one of their Midhampton boats would come in.

At approximately 3:00 p.m. the first of their boats came round the 'point,' and was immediately recognized. Harry Gibson's boat had made it. Harry came in slowly along the wharf, tied up the boat and climbed up the ladder at the side of the wharf.

His wife, who had worried for his safety from the time he had left the harbour greeted Harry. Sarah asked Harry Gibson if he had seen Ben. "No!" he replied, a bit surprised by the question and then Harry asked, "Is he out fishing?" Sarah then realised that Harry didn't know that Ben had gone to Dunkirk.

Harry last saw the *Syrup of Figs* tied up at the wharf when he left the harbour for Dunkirk. Sarah said, "Ben left for Dunkirk after you left." Mrs Tuck asked if Harry Gibson had seen her Walter. Harry replied, "Walter was about two hours behind. I knew it was him, I recognised his boat. He'll be here soon."

Almost to the minute, Walter's boat came around the 'point' and headed towards the harbour. He came up the ladder from his boat, unshaven, exhausted, and seemed to have aged years. Mrs Tuck hugged Walter. Her relief was evident. Mrs Tuck said to Walter, "Don't ever do such a thing again." He said, "No!" and meant it.

Two boats were now home with four more to come.

Another boat came round the 'point': Dick Bugler, the greengrocer. He seldom went far out to sea, always a bit nervous, but enjoyed what he had done, after he had thought about it. Dick was getting questioned about the others and the four boats yet to come. Dick said he could see the two boats behind him; he wasn't sure who they were, but they could be Jim Jesson and Bill Watson, their boats looked alike. He didn't really know if it was them. The fifth boat came in from further out to sea: Henry Ball, the lawyer. His boat travelled easily, skimmed the waves, until the engine was stopped, and then the boat was down in the water, slowly approaching the harbour.

Henry tied up his boat to the wharf and climbed up the ladder to face the same questions as had been asked of the others. He was more than surprised that young Ben had gone. He always liked Ben, who was always ready to help him with his boat, and always very polite.

Jim Jesson arrived soon after Henry. He was extremely tired and hungry, having no supplies left at all.

He didn't realise how far it was to Dunkirk, or the length of time he would be away. Only Ben was left to show up. Sarah, filled with disappointment, watched the 'point.' Fog was coming in early. Unless Ben arrived soon, he would surely get lost. Just before the fog nearly settled, another boat came around the 'point.' At first everyone thought it was Ben. Someone remarked, "That's not the *Syrup of Figs*." And it wasn't. It was the boat from

Penzance. People waiting on the pier were taken aback, at seeing the Cornish boat. The Cornishmen asked if they could tie up the boat. They were directed to a mooring, and were asking the local people for fuel. They were tall men; board-shouldered and quite tough looking. No one in their right mind would pick a fight with either. They were really gentle people, softly spoken. They were asked the same question by the people standing waiting, "Have you seen Ben Carter?" They had never heard of Ben Carter and enquired what he was like.

Someone said he was a boy who left here several days ago for Dunkirk.

"Ah! Yes, we saw him on our way out, sailing a boat with a funny name." Another in the crowd said, "*Syrup of Figs*?"

"He, told us there would most likely be diesel fuel available here."

"The last we saw of him, he was behind an old paddle wheeler, we never saw him again after that, but he was making good headway."

The Cornishman accent was different to the local dialect.

Ellen Carter spoke with them, telling them she was Ben's mother. Sarah was introduced to the Cornishmen and asked if they thought Ben would be all right. She told them that she and the family had heard that Ben had reached Dunkirk – but nothing since was heard.

The Cornishman assured Sarah and Ben's mother that he would be all right, but deep down they knew he may not make it. They had seen boats blown out of the water by the constant bombing and shelling – either boat could have been the *Syrup of Figs*.

Ellen invited the men from the Penzance for a meal and to meet Tom. They happily agreed, and after they arrived at the house, Tom told them that he had broken his ankle when he was about to leave for Dunkirk, but did not enlarge on the fact that Ben had left and taken the boat without telling anyone. Tom was pleased to meet them, and listened as they again related how they met up with Ben on the way to Dunkirk.

Ellen asked if the Cornishmen wanted to contact their families or anyone at home. They both said they had no telephone but perhaps they could contact the Penzance coast guard. They weren't familiar with telephones – other than having made a few local calls.

Tom volunteered to try and get through to the coast guard. He phoned the local exchange and asked for a trunk line for Penzance in Cornwall. He told the operator the call was very important. There must be people in Penzance who were as worried and concerned as he was about Ben.

The local operator told Tom to replace the phone and he would try and get the call through to the Penzance coast guard. About ten minutes went by, then Ben's grandmother, Rose and Sarah, came in. The phone rang and Tom quickly picked it up. Tom gave his name and explained, "I have two men from Penzance, who are making their way home from Dunkirk, here with me. Will you speak with them? Their names are George Robbins and Robert Trehayne." George spoke first and asked if he could let Mrs Robbins and his children know that he was at a small port about 100 miles west of Dover.

He said, "We have to stay here for a while. We had to come in for fuel." George handed the phone to Robert. Robert asked if he would please tell his family that he was all right. "I expect they are wondering where we are too." When speaking to one of their own, their accents became quite broad Cornish. The coast guard asked, "How long do you think it will be before you can get home?"

Robert said, "We plan to set out as early as possible in the morning. We have been told to keep south of the Isle of

54

Wight and, all being well, we should be by Portland Bill in early afternoon. Two more hours will take us past Start Point, and we should be home before dark, all being well." The coast guard told Robert how pleased he was to hear from them, and promised to get their messages delivered right away.

The two Cornishmen spent the night at the Carter's home. They had an early breakfast the following day and filled their boat tanks with fuel.

They asked Walter Tuck about the fog. He was waiting for Ben. Walter told them the fog would have lifted a couple of miles out, and they then decided to leave. Walter warned them to go early, as there were still a lot of boats heading west in the English Channel, and he didn't want them to have a collision. They said their 'goodbyes' and started the engine without difficulty. One of the Cornishmen engaged the propellers and slowly their boat pulled out of the harbour bound for Cornwall.

Ben sailed the boat out to keep away from any rocks that could be by the shore. The crowd waved farewell to Ben until he became a small speck fairly far out to sea and disappeared. Sergeant Dawson told the crowd that had assembled there on the beach what Ben had done. How he had so skilfully sailed the boat to and from Dunkirk.

Ben sat in his familiar position in the *Syrup of Figs*. He wanted so much to get home. He wondered how Sarah was, and his family, and Meg, his dog, who had looked so sad and broken-hearted when she was made to stay behind on the wharf with Sarah, instead of taking her usual trip.

It seemed a lifetime ago, when he had taken the *Syrup of Figs* out of harbour and headed for Dunkirk. The people who had met Ben on the beach, hearing he was short of food, gave him enough for a 'trip around the world'; including a large bottle of 'pop' and cases of fruit, and one lady even gave Ben a small ham. Ben opened a tin of peaches, which he loved. He was enjoying his food when he spotted two boats coming up behind him. As they got nearer Ben could see who they were. The boats were from Brixham, which he had seen on the way to Dunkirk. The boats were travelling faster than he was. Ben could see three men on each boat instead of two men on each boat. He had seen two men on each boat when he had last seen them. The men spotted Ben. They had thought about the boy in the boat that they had seen on the way to Dunkirk. They signalled to each other, pointing to Ben's boat. They slowed their engines and headed for the *Syrup of Figs*. They pulled along side and stopped. Ben stopped also. He was eating the last of his tins of peaches. They asked Ben if he had made it to Dunkirk, he said that he had.

The men saw the bullet holes in Ben's boat. They said they had been shot up too, and that they had lost one of their boats, just before getting to the beach in Dunkirk. They had saved the men in the third boat, hence three in each boat now. They asked Ben if he was able to bring anyone home. And when he said 'eleven,' they shook their heads in amazement. They had seen Ben eating his peaches, and asked him if he possibly had any food to spare. They had been able to get plenty of fuel at the port of Dover but no food. They had eked out their supply of food for the last two days but now had none left. Ben handed over as much as they required and more. He didn't want it, and had no need for the large amount he was given at the beach where he had landed the soldiers. He also gave them bottles of lemonade, and they starting eating straight away. Ben had never seen anyone that hungry before. They expressed gratitude for their unexpected supplies and left.

They hoped to get to Brixham by nightfall. Their motors soon drove their boats out of sight. They waved and were in awe of Ben, knowing what he had been through, amazed at the *Syrup of Figs* and that he had brought eleven men home.

Ben put the last of the petrol in the tank before starting up the Norton 500cc. He settled down and hoped to get home before dark. He wondered what his father would say. He had taken the boat when he shouldn't have and was now returning it with bullet holes in it.

At home Rose had trouble. Miss Taylor, Ben's schoolteacher, whom he disliked, was exercising her dog in Ben's field. Rose knew that Ben disliked her. Rose asked the policeman to stop Miss Taylor from exercising her dog in Ben's field. Rose didn't tell the policeman who owned the field – it didn't matter. Miss Taylor couldn't control the dog, which ran wild as soon as it was off the leash. The dog had been through the hedge several times into Ben's garden. It was a large dog and caused damage, as it raced through the seedlings.

It was mostly Labrador crossed with Alsatian. The policeman paid Miss Taylor a visit. He told her there had been a complaint about her going into the field, and letting her dog run loose. Miss Taylor told the policeman she would go when she wanted to go! "The dog didn't hurt anyone," she said. Again the policeman warned her not to go there with her dog, and left Miss Taylor's home. He didn't expect events to happen so fast.

When the constable left, Miss Taylor immediately took her dog and went straight to Ben's field. No one was going to tell her what to do. After all – she was a 'school teacher.' She thought she was better than anyone else. She had an idea who lodged the complaint. Miss Taylor went straight to the part of the field nearest the Carter garden.

Rose and Sarah were busy in the garden. Their thoughts never far from Ben, hoping he was all right. Meg was with them as, as usual, interested in what they were doing, content to listen to their chatter and at peace with the world.

Miss Taylor's dog broke through the garden hedge, grabbed Meg by the throat, and wouldn't let go.

Rose went immediately into action She grabbed a shovel and beat the intruder, which released Meg and the dog retreated back from where it had come. Sarah had never seen Rose so angry before. Rose went to the hedge, and told Miss Taylor she had no business to be in the field, to which Miss Taylor replied, "The field doesn't belong to you." Rose then said, "No it doesn't – it belongs to my grandson, Ben." Miss Taylor countered, "You don't tell the truth any better than your grandson." This statement upset Rose all over again.

Miss Taylor was told many 'home truths' during the conversation. She left the field and went directly to the police station. She told the policeman at the desk that she had seen Ben's grandmother beat off her dog – and to charge Rose with animal cruelty.

The magistrate was to hear the case at 10:30. The constable served the summons on Ben's grandmother that same evening, having seen the magistrate first. The magistrate was a retired judge, filling in for the justice department until a regular magistrate could be found.

Tom Carter called up his lawyer and solicitor who always dealt with his affairs. Mr Sparks, the lawyer, came round and went to the garden and saw the damage Miss Taylor's dog had caused. He saw the hole in the hedge where the dog broke through and heard the whole story. Mr Spark knew Ben owned the field, as he had helped with the transaction. He was well prepared now for the next morning.

Ben's family went to the Courthouse with Judge Dunne presiding as Magistrate. The Judge asked the charges to be heard. He then asked Rose how she pleaded and she replied, "Not guilty." Miss Taylor had a friend with her, another schoolteacher who looked the part. Rose took the stand and, on oath, related what had taken place.

The prosecution lawyer asked Rose if she had struck Miss Taylor's dog with a shovel and Rose replied, "Yes, I did."

Miss Taylor smirked – she thought she had won – she had taught the 'old girl' a lesson.

Rose stood down and Miss Taylor took her place. She swore to tell the truth and Mr Lawton started asking her questions. He asked her if she had taken her dog to the vet. She replied, "No I haven't. The dog is better, despite the terrible beating it had received from the defendant."

The elderly Judge watched Miss Taylor putting on an act. He remembered Rose. He had grown up at the same time, he had gone on to become a lawyer, and Rose married a local farmer. From time to time he heard about her.

The incident of a bunch of labourers hauling stone for a large house that was being built near their farm, using horses and carts, came to mind. The horses were expected to haul one ton of stone, on a cart from a quarry to the building site. After heavy rain the track they travelled on became a quagmire. One of the carts became stuck in the mud. Instead of taking off the stone to lighten the load, they tried to make the horse pull the whole load out of the mud. Grandmother Rose witnessed the horse taking a terrible beating, and tried to get help to stop the terrible cruelty. Rose asked two men to stop the men from beating the horse – but they were afraid to. There were at least a dozen men in the act. Eventually the horse collapsed and went down in the mud. Rose arrived on the scene. Her fury could not be contained. She went for them. One was stupid enough to order her away. She went after him with her stick that she had brought with her. She demanded a knife and the ruffian backed further away. One eventually gave her a heavy knife.

Rose cut off the harness, which had the horse fastened to the cart. She then went to the horse's head and knelt in the mud beside it. Speaking quietly to the horse Rose tried to get it to stand. The horse tried to understand that a human being could be gentle, and would not abuse and beat him. After several attempts the horse struggled to his feet. Blood was running from his injuries that had been inflicted upon him. Rose's fury had not abated. One of the men came forward to take hold of the horse's bridle. Rose, quick as lightening, hit him beside the head with her heavy stick and he went down in the mud.

Rose turned to the rest of the men who had been beating the horse and told them in strong tones, "You are the biggest bunch of bloody cowards on earth." A policeman had just arrived, having heard of the commotion. He asked Rose what was going on and, still hot with fury, she snapped, "Lock the cruel buggers up, and throw away the key."

Rose led the horse slowly away and looked after it until it was well. Its cuts had healed, and it had gradually settled down. It proved to be a gentle horse.

One day a man came to claim the animal. The news of the cruelty that had taken place had spread far and wide. He was nervous of going there after hearing what had happened. He asked her for the horse. Rose said "yes," he could take the horse. "But before you can take the animal I have something for you." Anticipating that Rose would produce her heavy stick, which had grown in size every time the story was told, he backed away. She gave him a bill for the care and upkeep of the horse. The amount added up to twice the value of the horse.

The man saw it and walked away saying, "You had better keep the animal." The horse stayed on the farm for the rest of its life.

Now here was Rose in court accused of cruelty by a trumped up school marm. The lawyer for Rose asked Miss Taylor if she had permission to go into the field.

"Has anyone ever told you not to go in there?" he asked. Miss Taylor replied, "Yes! The policeman said it – but I didn't do any harm."

"Did you have control over your dog when it attacked the Carter's dog?" the prosecution asked. She replied, "Yes!" Then she was asked, "Then why did you not stop the dog going into the Carter's garden?" Miss Taylor then said, "They had encouraged the dog over." Judge Dunne said, "You are under oath, Miss Taylor. Did you try and stop your dog from attacking their dog?" She said, "No!"

The lawyer turned to the Judge saying, "Do we need to take the case further? Rose Ellen only defended her grandson's dog, as anyone else would have done. She apparently did not hurt it or Miss Taylor would have taken it to a vet." The Judged agreed and dismissed the case.

Rose's lawyer addressed the Judge, "There is something else your Honour, to do with this case. Perhaps we could deal with it now?" The Judge said, "Yes! You have my permission." Rose's lawyer then read from a prepared statement. The court listened,

"The former defendant charges Miss Taylor with trespass upon her grandson's property; making a hole in the garden hedge of the Carter's property; causing destruction of a large amount of vegetables by letting her dog loose in the Carter's garden. I further charge her with deformation of character that Rose told lies like her grandson, without any foundation whatsoever. I apply for court costs on behalf of my client." Miss Taylor received a heavy fine, was forbidden to ever set foot on the Carter's property again, and was ordered to pay all costs. Rose didn't want her grandson to go back to school to face Miss Taylor ever again.

Ben knew nothing of this, obviously, as he had not returned from Dunkirk.

Ben began to feel tired, he relaxed. All he had to do was rest and steer the boat. He was used to hanging his arm over the handle, which held the rudder. The handle rested comfortable under his arm. Occasionally he glanced over his shoulder looking back east.

The last time he looked, he noticed a smudge of smoke. He remembered the paddle steamer from his trip on the way to Dunkirk. That was how he had first seen the boat that had helped him so much. Ben watched the boat draw nearer. He didn't realise he was being watched by the paddle steamer. The captain kept his binoculars trained on the *Syrup of Figs*. He remarked to his companion that he thought it was the same boat that had travelled in their wake, on the way to Dunkirk.

The afternoon sunshine was quite warm. Ben felt tiredness as he had never known before. He thought of home. Perhaps he would be there soon. Fifty miles should see him there. Ben decided to get behind the old ship, as he had done on the way to Dunkirk.

The ship was making good speed and was almost abreast of Ben when he made the decision. Travelling twenty miles behind the old paddle steamer would make his way a lot faster. Ben steered the *Syrup of Figs* toward the ship. The wake from the ship was close and he swung the *Syrup of Figs* straight towards it, as he had done before. He had spent several hours in that position, a hundred to a hundred-and-fifty yards behind the paddle wheeler. He could see the damage that had been done to the ship.

Later Ben heard that the paddle wheeler had made three trips to Dunkirk – at times under heavy fire.

The captain walked to the back of the ship. He waved to Ben, who waved back heartily. The captain was very pleased to see that Ben was all right. He had thought about the boy in the boat trailing his paddle wheeler on the way to Dunkirk. Now he knew he had made it. It seemed ages since he last saw the boat, when he had waved at him, over at Dunkirk, toward the beach.

Ben followed him for about two hours when he decided to get closer to land. The captain had left the position he had taken up in the back of the paddle wheeler. He now returned. He had wondered and worried where Ben's homeport was? Ben waved to him and pointed to the shore, changing course towards land. He rode the wave in the wake of the paddle wheeler, waved again to the captain and headed toward land.

Ben kept the direction toward shore until he was travelling parallel with the cliff about three miles out to sea. By six o'clock Ben was getting closer to home. Another two or three hours and he would be home.

The sun was beginning to set had already begun to drop behind the fog bank. Ben really disliked being out at sea in fog. He had been caught in it before and had been very lucky to get back to shore.

Ben now had to make a decision to land on the shore somewhere, or risk being caught in the fog. Ben chose to land early and would continue when the fog had lifted. Then Ben remembered the small beach that his father and the family had used to take him for trips. He decided he would try and find his way there. The change of plan meant that Ben had to get close to shore so that he could pick a safe place to land. He slowed the motor when he was about two hundred yards off the beach, and eventually came to the place he was looking for.

Ben slowed the boat and went straight in. The tide was at its highest. The previous high tide had left the usual line of seaweed and flotsam. The new high tide had just reached that line.

Ben cut the motor, and the boat drifted forwards and

touched the shingle. Ben hopped over the front and pulled as hard as he could on the rope. A few small waves hit the back of the *Syrup of Figs* driving it a bit further up the beach.

Ben remembered the log, or part of a tree that had washed in by the sea. It had become embedded in the shingle. Ben tied the *Syrup of Figs* to the log. He was quite unsteady on his feet. The time he had spent at sea on this trip was far longer than any trip before. Ben took some of the food, which had been given to him from the boat, when he was on the beach with the soldiers.

The fog had got really thick by now. To continue now would have been impossible. He was suffering from tiredness and near exhaustion, which would have made him more likely to make mistakes.

Ben finished his meal. He took the tarpaulin from the boat, and dragged it up to the base of the cliff – the pebbles were still warm from the day's sunshine. Ben lay on one half of the tarp and pulled the other half over him. Every effort he made seemed to take the last of his energy. Sleep came easily. He knew he had about twelve hours, before the tide went out and came back in – which would enable him to launch the *Syrup of Figs* to sail the last miles for home.

It was now more than a day since the last boat had returned to Midhampton from Dunkirk. Six boats had made it, all of them had brought back grateful soldiers. The six boats had made land at different points along the coast to discharge their cargo of grateful soldiers. None of them had seen Ben or the *Syrup of Figs*.

At Midhampton, people had waited all day down at the wharf hoping that Ben would appear. Sarah had waited. Sometime her mother joined her, and sometimes Ben's mother had waited with her – no sign of the *Syrup of Figs*. They saw several boats, further out to sea, travelling west, but the number of boats became fewer as the day wore on. No other boat came into the small harbour.

The fog settled in at evening time as it often did at this time of year. They knew Ben wouldn't be able to navigate through the fog, even if he had survived to come this far. All were beginning to face the fact that Ben could be lost.

Sarah said a prayer, not a Jewish or a Christian prayer just: "Please God – send home Ben."

The following day – Sunday – the Carter's went to church, joined by Sarah, David and Ruth Bennett. The fog was still bad, and was as thick as ever. No hope for Ben to come in – even if he was able to come.

Ben awoke and looked at his watch – he had slept for just over twelve hours. The tide had gone out, and was now lapping the *Syrup of Figs*. Ben decided he had to launch the boat or else he would be there for another twelve hours. Ben tried to think what day it was. After getting his mind together, he realised it was his birthday. He was now fourteen years old – the magic number. By law, he didn't have to attend school anymore. No more Miss Taylor if he could leave.

Ben had no way of knowing what had transpired in his absence. The fog was still dense. Ben decided to lay offshore after he had launched the *Syrup of Figs* and wait for the sun to burn off the fog.

With much effort the *Syrup of Figs* was afloat. Ben took her out far enough to be in sight of the beach. The tide wasn't strong, Ben just had to wait.

By 8:30 a.m. Ben saw the sun break through the thick blanket of fog. He waited another half an hour then he started the Norton 500cc for the last part of the trip.

He sailed straight out from shore for about half a mile, then headed west. He knew where he was, despite there still being patches of fog. After a while, about three miles

65

from home, Ben sailed into thick fog again. He turned out to sea. The fog was fairly coastal, and low; further out Ben could begin to see landmarks he was familiar with.

Just showing above the fog – he could see the tip of a fir tree by his field. He lined the tree up with the farmyard in the distance and slowly followed the line between the two points. To the east he picked up another landmark he used the church spire in the distance in the next village to where Ben lived, and another farm in line with it. When both lines were visible, and in line he knew exactly where he was.

He could go into the harbour easily from where he was.

Tom Cater sat in his wheelchair. Rose was with him and their thoughts were with Ben, wherever he was. Meg was lying in her usual place beside the wheelchair. Rose was the first to notice that Meg became uneasy. She lifted her head, her ears went up and she listened intently. Tom and Rose watched her, wondering what was bothering her. Suddenly Meg leapt to her feet and headed for the open door. She ran down the street as fast as she could go, barking all the way. Ellen Carter and Sarah and her parent's were at church. The church was packed with people, as it had been in recent weeks. The Vicar, instead of church rituals, gave thanks for the safe return of the men in the six boats that had returned and the soldiers they had brought with them. He asked a special prayer for Ben and his family.

Everyone in the church heard Meg barking. She went tearing by the church still barking. The church door was open, and they thought a dog had been hurt or was in some kind of distress.

Sarah realised it was Meg who was barking. She whispered to Ellen, "That sounds like Meg." The two of them quietly left their pews and the church and several people followed.

Meg had gone down to the wharf. She had heard the unmistakable beat of the Norton 500cc engine, which had taken Ben on his long trip in the *Syrup of Figs*.

Rose brought Tom to the wharf in his wheelchair. They too could see the boat that was now in full view. Sarah shouted, "He's home!"

Ben pulled the boat into the wharf. Eager hands helped him tie up the *Syrup of Figs*. Ben climbed the ladder up the side of the wharf to be greeted first by Sarah and his family. Ellen, with tears of joy running down her cheeks said, "Happy Birthday Ben. Thank God you came home."

Rose greeted Ben. She was worried silently – her worry had turned to despair – she had resigned herself to the real possibility that Ben was not coming home. She stepped forward to Ben's side and hugged him, and said, "Thank God you are home."

Ben walked over to his father who was sitting in his wheelchair. From time to time Ben had worried what Tom would say when he saw that the *Syrup of Figs* now had bullet holes in it? Tom had been anxiously waiting for so long for Ben's return, he didn't care what damage it had received, as long as the boy got home. Tom said, "Well done son. Welcome home and Happy Birthday!"

The small party walked to Ben's home. The crowd of people who had been watching, parted to make way for them, and gave Ben a big 'cheer' and 'congratulations.'

Ben was still a bit unsteady on his feet. When they arrived back at the Carter home, Ben stayed for a while, answering questions, and then left with Sarah to see the garden. The roses were in bloom – the place looked so peaceful.

Rose joined the two of them. Coming from her cottage. She had seen them in the garden, and came over and joined in the conversation. Sarah and Rose had worked hard to keep the garden in order while Ben was away. Despite the twelve hours sleep Ben had had on the beach he was still extremely tired. He went in and had a light meal and went to bed, where he had imagined to be many times on the way to Dunkirk and back, when he had felt so desperately tired.

Ellen woke Ben for breakfast after he had slept for fourteen hours. Sarah came around for a visit. She had skipped school to be with Ben.

Tom asked some questions of Ben about having talked to the Cornishmen Ben had met at sea. Tom had a pretty good idea what Ben had been through. Ben described how he followed the paddle steamer, which they had seen at Weymouth.

The paddle steamer had become quite famous after her three trips to Dunkirk. The last trip had been the worse. German planes bombed and machine-gunned non-stop. The RAF had done their possible best – fighting off the planes.

The German artillery was now in range, and they too had fired on the ship. The old paddle wheeler was hit several times, but managed to load soldiers on board. The ship was packed, and more and more added, somehow squeezing on a few more men. The captain ordered as much power as he could get. The weight of humanity on board had the paddle steamer way down in the water. The wind of the fan, which blew the furnace of the engine, doubled the consumption of coal. One of the stokers remarked that the boiler would blow up, to which he was answered, "If we stay around here in Dunkirk, we'll be blown up by the Germans." The result of the extra steam gave the captain more power to use – which he did.

The wheels on each side of the boat spun faster than ever before – pushing the boat out of the harbour and eventually out of harms way.

For several miles the old steam engine drove the ship. The boiler was still red-hot, large amounts of water were converted to steam. The order eventually came from the captain to return to normal running, to the great relief of the stokers, exhausted from shovelling coal into the engine.

The boiler lost its red glow and all was well. They made it to Dover to be told that the evacuation from Dunkirk was over.

The ships, big and small, had brought home 325,000 men. All the boats had taken part in a miracle: "The miracle of Dunkirk."

Ben, Sarah, Mr and Mrs Carter and Rose were having supper and talking about the war as most people were. Everybody knew England was in a desperate position. Winston Churchill warned of the situation ahead for the nation. Britain was going to fight on.

The Bennett family could not see how Britain, so ill prepared, could withstand the German onslaught. Their prospects didn't bear thinking about if the Germans conquered Britain. Neither could they understand, like the majority of other British people, why America didn't enter the war. Their ambassador, Kennedy, advised Roosevelt not to give Britain any help, because, in his opinion, he thought Britain would surely loose the war.

The Bennett's could not understand the British; no other nation on earth would rescue such a large army from certain defeat, as they had done in Dunkirk. They heard that more than 700 boats had taken part in the evacuation.

David and Ruth Bennett asked Tom Carter and some of his associates, "How can Britain possibly win this war in face of such odds?" Tom spoke for them all, "I don't know how we will win – but we will win."

David thought, 'what an incredible race the British are,' and David was somewhat assured.

As the war progressed he never heard anyone say that they thought Britain would lose.

The pro-German American ambassador was sent home.

After Dunkirk German planes began attacking Britain in increasing numbers. Already the RAF was having success against them.

There was a knock at the Carter's front door. Someone wanted to see Ben. Ellen answered the door, asked the man, a Mr Roper, to come in. Mr Roper said he was the former owner of the field Ben had purchased. He nodded and wished Ben's grandmother Rose, "Good day!" Rose had known him all her life. Mr Roper said, "I hear you put the school teacher in her place. I always had trouble keeping folks out of that field. I expect this court business will put a stop to it. I had plans for that field, but I haven't been well for a while – so that is why I decided to sell. The reason why I came in is that I still have a tractor I bought two-years ago, and wondered if Ben would like it? There is a plough and harrows with it, and several others implements as well."

Ben was interested – he wanted to start cultivating the field. Ben knew the tractor, an Allis Chalmers. It was just the right size. Ben was a bit uneasy dealing in front of his family. Rose suggested at one point getting a horse to do the work. Ben was not keen on the idea.

Mr Roper said he would like to see the roses in the garden that he had heard about. Ben asked Sarah to accompany them.

When they reached the garden and had seen the lovely roses, Ben asked Mr Roper what price he had in mind for the tractor and the equipment. Mr Roper said he hoped for a hundred pounds; he thought that was a fair price. Ben took Sarah's hand, drew her a short distance away, and asked her what she thought about the purchase. Sarah knew very little about tractors, but she said it sounded all right. She nodded to Ben, "Yes!"

They walked back to where Mr Roper was standing, and told him that they would purchase what he had offered, for his price.

Mr Roper said, "There is a good trailer which I have included in the sale, not a big trailer, but not too small for the tractor and the trailer has rubber tires." Mr Roper then left. Ben and Sarah went back into the house and announced that they had come to a deal.

The following morning Sarah and Ben went to examine what they had agreed to purchase. They were pleased at the condition of the tractor and the implements.

Ben paid Mr Roper, loaded up the trailer with the implements and started up the tractor. Mr Roper promised to help Ben set up the plough when he was ready.

Ben drove the tractor home across town, even coming down the main street. Sarah insisted that they stopped at the Taylor's shop – to show her parents, who pretended to be impressed. They asked themselves, "What would be next?"

The policeman stopped to look over Ben's tractor, commenting what a good tractor it was. He added, "How did you get here?" Ben replied he had driven it from Mr Roper's farm. The police constable asked Ben if he could see his licence. Ben had to admit that he did not have one. He hadn't given a licence a thought, and added that he was sorry. The constable knew Ben, and the great journey to Dunkirk he had made. He said, "You get back on the tractor and drive it carefully home, and don't drive it on the highway again until you have a licence."

Ben and Sarah drove home, subdued. Early in the afternoon they went out to haul the lobster traps. They had a good catch. They re-baited the traps and put them down again in the sea. On the way home they spotted a shoal of mackerel. The *Syrup of Figs* lay in the water with no engine running. They drifted slowly with the tide. Soon they caught the largest amount of fish they had ever landed, and then they headed home. They unloaded their catch on the wharf and were on their way home. Ben pushed what he called the fish-cart, laden with various fish. There was an air battle developing over the channel. The noise of gunfire reminded Ben of Dunkirk.

Sarah and Ben saw a plane coming down, smoke coming from behind it.

They watched in horror as the plane headed towards the sea. They saw the pilot climb out and jump, or fall, from the plane. His parachute opened and he dropped in the sea – about a mile out. Ben left his barrow of fish and lobsters, and run back to the *Syrup of Figs* which was tied to the wharf. He undid the ropes, and started the engine. Sarah dropped into the boat, Ben protested that she shouldn't come. She said, "I'm not letting you out of my sight – or you'll be gone again." Ben opened the throttle to full speed. The *Syrup of Figs* went out of the harbour faster than it had ever done before. It bucked some of the waves, and slammed into some of the others – but Ben didn't slacken speed. He headed for the position where he had last seen the pilot before he disappeared into the sea. Ben estimated that five minutes would take them to the spot. After a couple of minutes, Ben could see, to his relief, the pilot in the water. Ben steered towards him, and slackened speed just before he reached the pilot. The pilot was tangled in his parachute. Ben reached over the side of the boat and got hold of the pilot's arm.

The pilot was not a large man but it still took Ben and Sarah's combined strength to get him on board even after cutting off the parachute he was entangled everything had happened so fast. A few minutes ago, Ben was on the wharf with Sarah.

Ben asked the pilot if he was hurt or wounded. The pilot replied, "Another minute and I would have gone under – I couldn't have held out much longer." Ben headed back for the harbour. This was the first of many who would crash into the sea in the autumn of 1940.

The *Syrup of Figs* arrived at the wharf. The ambulance and doctor had just arrived and the pilot was taken into the ambulance. He thanked Ben and Sarah profusely before leaving. Ben's fish barrow was still there where he had left it, a short while ago.

After events such as this, people often say 'if this or that hadn't happened, things would turn out differently.'

If Ben and Sarah hadn't stopped to fish they would have been home earlier. They could not have responded to the event as they did – and the pilot would have been lost.

People who came onto the wharf after the plane had crashed – purchased all the fish and lobster Ben and Sarah had caught. Ben thought to himself 'not too bad a day after all'. 'Lightening' struck twice in that day as another plane went down further out to sea than the last. Ben and Sarah were ready to go fishing again when again they saw a pilot coming down. Ben started the *Syrup of Figs* and headed out to sea again. Before the pilot dropped into the water the *Syrup of Figs* was well on the way.

They spotted the pilot, and pulled along side were he was floundering in the sea. This rescue was different. He was not RAF, he was a German. Ben and Sarah were both bewildered they never had expected to come face-to-face with one of the people who were portrayed as monsters.

Ben, although he had been to Dunkirk and back, had never seen a German before. The man was asking for help in the German language. Sarah spoke to him in fluent German, to his surprise. They pulled him on board their boat, and headed back to harbour.

Sarah had helped save one of the German race who

were killing her people. She didn't say any more until the pilot was handed over to the authorities at the wharf. She said then to the German, "You can tell your people you were saved by a Jewish girl. For the rest of your life, remember your life depended on a Jew."

The German pilot said nothing. 'Thank you' was not in his vocabulary – not even in German it seemed.

Ben and Sarah were congratulated for what they had done. Their efforts had saved the lives of two airmen – even if one was the enemy.

They then went home to the Carter house, and received more congratulations. Ben and Sarah hadn't realised that Meg had been with them for each rescue trip. She had jumped on board without being noticed, because of the excitement.

Meg always came out when there were crew to rescue.

David and Ruth Bennett were dismayed to hear Ben and Sarah had rescued a German. They had good reason. English people now rescued the Germans who had destroyed their way of life in Germany. They thought for a while, they had received papers to say they were now British subjects. And that their future was assured. The Bennett's has prospered since coming to England. Their only daughter, Sarah, was happy with the life. They would be forever reminded of what would have happened to them had they not escaped Germany when they did, but they would try to be British. What was to become of Sarah? They didn't know – but they had a pretty good idea.

The Battle of Britain was raging. The RAF was more than holding its own against the German onslaught. If they had lost the Battle of Britain Germany would try and invade England.

More people from the British Empire and Commonwealth were arriving.

The Bennett's still could not quite grasp why so many

from Australia and New Zealand had come half way around the world to fight for a country they had never seen.

Some Americans still said, and thought, that Britain would lose the war, especially the Kennedy's, who seemed to be on Hitler's side.

Ben went to see Mr Roper. He ploughed up part of his field. Mr Roper came, as promised, and set up the plough on the tractor. The plough had only one furrow, but quite an area was now ploughed. Rose came to watch, forever interested in the business she knew so well. Rose scooped up some soil with her bare hands, looked at it carefully, with satisfaction.

Ben could sell everything he grew. His produce was of the highest standard and he needed more land to grow more.

Ben harrowed the land he had ploughed and eventually planted the area to vegetables. He purchased some chickens, which were kept in the barn. Here again, demand for eggs was greater than production. Rose helped and was happy to take part in something like her old life, and put in part of her wealth of knowledge to Ben and Sarah.

Gradually the flock of chickens grew. Ben did not go back to school. He said he was old enough to leave school, as he was fourteen.

The headmaster of his school came to visit, but no amount of persuading could change Ben's mind. The headmaster said, unwisely, that Ben would never make anything of his life.

Rose Ellen normally said nothing but wouldn't let the headmaster get away with that. She snapped, "I'll wager Ben would not trade his bank account with yours, and I doubt you had the guts to sail a boat to Dunkirk," and added, "you have no more intelligence than that teacher,

Taylor, you hired."

Rose left the house in a very hostile mood. The headmaster left also, wishing that he had never come.

Tom and Ellen had spoken to a retired university professor about Ben leaving school. The old professor said that Ben was very bright. "He used to sell me some of his produce, and showed me how I can grow my own," adding, "if Ben will agree to it, I will teach him, whenever he would like to come around to see me. Ben hasn't too much time on his hands, with this large garden. And going to sea tending his lobster traps but you will be surprised what can be achieved if Ben is agreeable."

The Carter's explained to Ben that, if he left school, he would have to go and see the professor to be tutored. Ben said, "Anything would be better than school; no more Miss Taylor; no more bullies and no more teachers." Then Ben agreed. Now came a problem. Sarah! She didn't want Ben to leave school. They had gone to school together, ever since she came from Germany. She told her parents that Ben was leaving school, and she wanted to leave school too.

David and Ruth said, "No!" She had to go to school. Sarah said, "No! I'm not going to school, I'm going to leave school and help Ben." Sarah was adamant. She left the house in tears, and went straight to see Ben, who was upset to see Sarah so distressed. Ben asked her what the problem was, and, between sobs, told Ben her parents would not let her leave school.

Grandmother Rose was in the garden with Ben. She heard what had happened at Sarah's home, and made a suggestion. "You know Professor Brooks will tutor Ben, why shouldn't he be asked to teach Sarah at the same time." Rose left them and went into the house to tell Tom and Ellen.

Rose said, "Since coming here to live, I have done my

best not to interfere in the family, and I apologise for speaking out of turn to Ben's headmaster," and added again, "no wonder Ben wanted to get out of the place." Rose continued, "Sarah is in the garden with Ben. She wants to leave school. Her parents will not let her leave – hence she's upset." Rose suggested to Tom and Ellen what she had proposed to Ben and Sarah. If Mr Brooks will teach them, he is far better educated than any of those teachers that those two have had to put up with." Both Tom and Ellen said they couldn't interfere in Sarah's family's decisions, but Tom did agree to see Mr Brooks. Then he would go along to see the Bennett's. Rose was leaving. She turned around and said, "I'll try not to interfere again, but I hope you will try – for Ben and Sarah's sake. They have never been apart since Sarah arrived, and maybe they never will be."

Tom and Ellen walked down the road to Mr Brooks' cottage, just as the sun was going down. Mr Brooks was at home, and invited them in. They had never been in his home before. There were books everywhere, neatly packed on shelves. Tom thought 'I suppose that was to be expected.'

Tom repeated Rose's request that they visit, and asked Mr Brooks if he would tutor Sarah as well as Ben. Ben and Sarah had always been inseparable since Sarah had arrived in England. Mr Brooks agreed commenting, "I often see them working in the garden. In fact, if you ever see one then the other is not far away. Yes I will teach them both." Mr Brooks went on to say, "My life has been quite empty since I retired, and my dear wife passed away two years ago, as you know, so it will help me too. It will give me something to live for again."

Tom asked Mr Brooks what he would like to be paid for his services and he said, "Ben has helped me with my garden and he would never take anything for his help, despite my trying to give him something for his labour, and so neither will I. They will be doing something in return, anyway, their company will mean a lot to me."

Mr Brooks walked with Tom and Ellen to the Bennett's home. It was fairly late in the day now. But they had not gone to bed yet. They were still upset that Sarah wanted to leave school, wondering where she had gone, but they had a good idea.

The proposition was put to the Bennett's. Mr Brooks spoke of his experience teaching at one of the best universities in England. The Bennett's readily agreed with the plan, for a couple of reasons: one was that Ben and Sarah would get a good education – the other was that they didn't have much alternative.

Ben and Sarah were working in the garden. Ben was putting his tractor in the barn when his father and mother came. Mr and Mrs Bennett and Mr Brooks were with them. Tom asked Ben to go to his grandmother's house and ask her to come over,

Rose arrived in due course, anxiously looking from one to the other. Rose was introduced to Mr Brooks, and she had heard of him but had never met him.

After some light conversation, Tom spoke about Ben and Sarah's education. He said, "Mr Brooks has agreed to tutor them both, if they are in agreement. On the condition that they go to Mr Brooks' home when opportunities come to do so, for example, on wet days or in the evening times, or when no work can be done in the garden. And any time when Ben and Sarah have to go to sea they will be excused." They all agreed, no more school. If Ben had gone back to school then Horsefall and Bakey would not have left them alone. Ben was getting very strong for his age, and could take care of himself. Unfortunately, bullies usually became prefects and had too much authority. Rose was pleased with the arrangement and said so.

Tom then had an idea. He asked his mother-in-law, Rose, to be responsible for seeing the young people went to Mr Brooks when they were able. Rose looked at Ben and Sarah – her pride and joy – and said she would. All was well on the education front.

Ben and Sarah walked in the flower garden. Night had taken over, the fragrance of the flowers more pungent with darkness. They enjoyed the moment. The garden was so peaceful and quiet – no one could imagine there being a war on.

The following day a plane crashed into the sea. Ben and Sarah were in their field. They dropped their tools and raced for the wharf. Meg had got there first. Ben started the motor as Sarah untied the mooring ropes. They headed out of the harbour at full speed. The plane had not sunk as they normally did, fairly quickly.

The pilot was in his cockpit. Ben eased the *Syrup of Figs* toward the front of the plane. He stopped the engine and they set about pulling the man out of the aircraft. Ben had become quite expert at getting straps etc. released in order to release pilots from parachutes, Ben soon had him free – and the pilot was pulled out of the plane with difficulty. The aircraft was now sinking – and it was a race against time. Eventually they managed to get the pilot into the boat. Ben and Sarah were concentrating so hard on what they were doing, they did not realise by the time the pilot was onboard the *Syrup of Figs* that the airman had died.

Ben had seen dead soldiers at Dunkirk, but he wasn't prepared for this. Sarah backed away in horror. She had never seen a dead person before.

They reached the harbour feeling very low in spirits. Ben remarked, "If only we had had a faster boat, we may have been able to save him." Sarah replied, "We did our best – we couldn't have done any more."

They arrived at the wharf. People had gathered, as they usually did, relieved that the pilot had been rescued, but were shocked to find that he had died.

After the pilot had been taken away, Ben approached Mr Gibson and Walter Tuck. They too had been rescuing aircrew from the sea. Ben told them he thought he could have saved the pilot had he been there sooner. There was some discussion between them. Mr Gibson said he had heard the RAF were placing boats along the coast, in various harbours.

Ben remembered seeing one of the RAF boats approaching him a week before, when he had rescued a pilot. The RAF boat was based too far away, and further along the coast, so could not reach the pilot as quickly as the *Syrup of Figs*.

Mr Gibson suggested he contact the RAF Air Sea Rescue Service. He did this, and explained the situation to them. He pointed out the need for one of their faster boats in this area. He also suggested that the boat be manned by local people. The volunteers were all boat owners who had been to Dunkirk and they knew that part of their coast better than anyone else. The officer in charge of the Air Sea Rescue Service promised to reply to Mr Gibson as soon possible. He said he understood the problem, and realised a lot of air battles were taking place over them.

As a result of the meeting the RAF sent an officer of the Air Sea Rescue organisation to meet the boat owners who were volunteering their time and services, all of which had made the round trip to Dunkirk.

They met at the Gibson's home. There was discussion about the speed at which the boats could be send out from the harbour, and the need of a much faster boat to get to the downed aircrew.

There was also a request made for a manned coast guard station to co-ordinate the rescue operations.

Ben agreed to man the boat with Sarah – making eight people available. Two would be on standby, taking it in turn. This would mean the boat could set out immediately if there was a need. The officer questioned whether Ben and Sarah were old enough to take on such a demanding task. Mr Gibson answered, "Ben went to Dunkirk, on his own – no one asked him to go and he was able to bring back eleven soldiers in a seventeen foot boat." He added, "Ben and Sarah have rescued more aircrew than any of the others."

The officer then asked about the children missing school. They replied that they were being tutored by a university professor, and were doing well, to everyone's satisfaction.

The officer referred to a document he had with him, and after a while spoke again. "If you all feel you can handle a faster boat – I know where there is one. We are desperately short of manpower; the boat will have to be fetched from its present location by you. When the rescue boat gets here you will be instructed on how to use and maintain it. I will also arrange for you to be picked up from here and taken to Poole Harbour in Dorset, where the boat is in dock.

"I will also arrange for a coast guard station for this area with ship-to-shore radio for the boat. Thank you for all you have done to save the lives on this part of the coast."

"I would like two volunteers to bring the boat from Poole to here."

Walter Tuck was first to put his name forward. There was some hesitation from the rest. Ben's life was pretty full, he would have loved to have gone but he was extremely busy in the garden. Being tutored and having agreed to the latter took up most of his time.

The men all remembered their trips to Dunkirk. They

would do it again, but preferred not to make any more long trips if they could avoid it.

Walter asked Ben if he would go. Before he could answer, Sarah said forcefully, "If he goes – I go. He's not going to do what he did when he went out to Dunkirk, when he left me behind." She burst into tears at the thought of it. The officer was taken aback – he had never met a more determined young lady.

Ben reluctantly agreed to go, and agreed to take Sarah. The officer continued, "The engine of that boat is very powerful, and capable of driving through the sea at very high speeds. In fact, I think it has a Rolls Royce engine. A car will be sent tomorrow morning. The air battles are going to get a lot worse, and the need for Air Sea Rescue will be greater. Every pilot we save is imperative to the war effort. Your route from Poole to here will be planned for you, and priority given to your passage."

Ben and Sarah went to visit Mr Brooks, to inform him of the plans that were made for them and to say that they wouldn't be around for their tutoring until they arrived back home.

The next morning a car arrived to pick them up, as the officer had promised, driven by an RAF driver.

Tom, Ellen Rose and the Bennett's gathered to see them off and wish them a safe return. They travelled over the road that they had taken when they went to Weymouth the day that war was declared. The driver didn't talk too much, but he was pleasant.

They were interested in the countryside as they went by. They made their way to Southampton then went along the coast road past Portsmouth and on to Poole. Upon arriving there they were given a meal.

Walter Tuck had never been to Poole before, and was especially interested in the flying boat. Two were just leaving for their long trip over the Atlantic – huge

Sunderland planes specially equipped for coastal command.

The next surprise was that they were told they had to wear uniforms – by International Law. Anyone serving in the Armed Forces had to wear a uniform. Sarah would have to wear a man's outfit, as there were no female uniforms available for her at that time. One would be issued to her later, when it was available.

Walter, Sarah and Ben had expected to leave soon after arriving but they had to be made familiar with the new boat. They were taken to see her. The boat was larger than any of them expected – and obviously built for speed. They were shown over the boat's small engine room, and various things necessary for rescuing aircrew from the sea. The medical locker contained morphine, and was locked. The key was given to Walter, as he was the oldest, and expected to be the most responsible.

There was a ship-to-shore radio and a provision had been made so the operator of the boat could speak to aircraft and listen to any aircraft in the vicinity of the boat.

They were taken to a building where they changed into their uniforms, which fitted fairly well, but Sarah's was tight in places, she being larger in places where the men were not.

The fuel tank of the boat was full and ready to go. Another RAF officer came and instructed them about the rapid accelerating mechanism. He started the engine and eased slowly forward the small arm, which controlled the accelerator. They drove around the harbour for awhile – each getting familiar with the speed of the boat, and how easy it was to manoeuvre. The new boat had a reverse – which would be of great help.

The twin propellers were quite large. There was a flag flying at the front of the boat – the red, white and blue circle of the Royal Air Force. They were ready to go.

Some food was packed and put on board, mineral water and tins of fruit. They were all set.

Walter turned to Ben and said, "You take her out!" Ben started the engine, opened up the throttle and, slowly at first, headed towards home.

They had all been advised which route to take. There would be ships going in and out of the ports of Southampton and Portsmouth, "But not too much after that – most boats will let you pass without hindrance, but the larger ships can't, you have to avoid them," he was told.

Ben increased speed. He realised the tremendous power of the new boat. H never expected to be on such a large boat, and certainly not in charge of one.

They were now parallel with the coast heading east. A few hours ago they were going west, parallel to the sea, in the officer's car. The throttle was only open a quarter of the way, and they were already travelling faster than any of them had ever been. Even so, at the speed they were going, it would mean they wouldn't arrive back at Midhampton before dark.

Ben increased speed again – the response from the engine was immediate. The sea was fairly calm and the boat cut through the water with ease.

The speed was increased again to three-quarters, and again there was a quick response. Ben didn't risk going any faster until he had become familiar with the boat. The engine was surprisingly quiet – they could hear each other easily, without raising their voices.

Ben offered Walter the chance to drive for a while – which he agreed to do. Ben handed the wheel over, and went to the side of the boat. Sarah was standing there watching the waves go by. Ben stood beside her. He too watched for a while when without thinking or forethought he put his hand around Sarah's waist. She was taken aback – but still watched the sea. They turned and faced each other, closer than they have ever been before. They had been together for several years but this was the first time that they were this close. From then on things would be different in many ways. They were both growing into adults with all that that would entail.

Sarah was blushing as she said to Ben, "I have been waiting for you to do that for a long while."

The RAF boat travelled easily at speed. The front came up. The faster it went. Hopefully they would be home before dark. Ben and Sarah had never been happier. Sarah left Ben's side, went forward, and handed round the food that had been put there for them. They were ready for a meal. They were excited and pleased with their new acquisition. When aircrew landed in the water they could now reach them quickly.

Ben again took a turn at the wheel. Walter was well pleased. If he had the wheel of the *Queen Mary* he couldn't have been prouder than at the wheel of the new boat.

The wind had ceased, which meant that fog would develop along the coast. Walter estimated that, if all went well they should be home in an hour.

Sarah took a turn next at steering. She opened the engine up to full speed with the others approval. The boat was now skimming the water. She kept the speed up at full throttle, heading toward the harbour, and covering the last nautical miles home.

Tom, Ellen and Rose went down to the wharf, pretty sure the three would be home that evening, as planned. The other men who had volunteered to man the boat were there too, as well as a few other interested citizens – all watching toward the west.

David Bennett was first to see the new rescue boat quite a way out to sea – it was moving at high speed. The boat turned easily and headed towards them. It was the boat they had been waiting for.

Sarah was still at the wheel. She cut the speed to less than a quarter and brought the new boat into the harbour, getting slower, and eventually stopping altogether, pulling to that part of the wharf where the boat was moored. All present were pleased to see the trio, and very were interested in the boat, the fastest ever, to come into the harbour.

The Bennett family were especially proud that Sarah had brought her in. The crowd dispersed after a while, and went their separate ways.

Ben and Sarah had to see to something in the garden – so went back to the Carter home. They walked in silence. As Ben walked with Sarah he was deep in thought. When they arrived at the Bennett's home, Ben turned to Sarah and he placed his hands on her shoulders pulled her gently towards him and kissed her for the first time.

Sarah looked at Ben – surprised, but she had expected something to happen. She slipped her arms around Ben's neck and kissed him again. She said, "Goodnight Ben – thank you!"

Ben left. He thought he was walking on air. He realised too, that they were no longer friends like they used to be. Something far stronger had taken the place of friendship.

Before going into the house Ben walked around the rose garden. He was at peace with the world, but couldn't imagine what the world held for him. When he entered the house his parents and Rose were there waiting. Anxious to hear of the day's events, they sat down and listened to Ben's story of the day's happenings.

He told them all the operators of the new rescue boat had to wear uniforms when operating the new boat when in operations and why.

Ben went to his room, and eventually to bed. His thoughts were of Sarah, and he asked himself where the 'friendship' was going. He was eventually overcome by sleep. What a day it had been.

The next morning, after a good breakfast the shop was open as usual. Ben walked next door to see his grandmother. Rose seemed sad and Ben asked if something was troubling her. She said she had a dream last night of 'Sweetwater Farm', that she was back there living, and when she awoke of course it wasn't true. Ben stayed awhile, and she eventually cheered up back to her normal self.

She told Ben to be very careful with the new boat. Ben left Rose's home and walked down to the wharf to be with the rest of the Dunkirk veterans. They listened intently to Walter Tuck explaining how everything worked and what had been explained to Walter, Ben and Sarah at Poole by the RAF instructor who had shown them, also the experience they had gained by bringing the boat back to the harbour.

They made an agreement that each would exchange turns with Ben, Sarah and Walter, in manoeuvring the boat. Harry Gibson would go with Walter. Another would go with Ben and Sarah in turn, until all became familiar with the capabilities of the new craft.

Sarah thought the boat should have a name. There was already a number painted quite large on the boat. A name would give it a bit of dignity they all agreed. Several names were suggested but Harry said, "I don't think it should have a feminine name. How about naming it the *Syrup of Figs II*. It had been Ben's idea to get a faster boat, and I think that would be appropriate." They all agreed. There was now a new *Syrup of Figs*.

Later on in the day, a plane went down offshore. The pilot managed to parachute into the sea. The new *Syrup of Figs II* was called on, for the first time, to try to save a pilot. Walter Tuck took the first mission. Four of the others jumped in beside him in the boat, which streaked out to sea. They were not too far offshore when they picked up the RAF pilot. He was thankful to have been picked up so quickly. The *Syrup of Figs II* was ideally suited to do what she was called on to do, and she repeated the performance many more times for friend and foe alike.

The friendship between Ben and Sarah had changed. They were more reserved somehow, no longer the happy carefree days working together. Something deeper had developed without them realising what was happening. They were only 14 years old, but age didn't matter. There was little time between Mr Brooks' lessons, and the expanding flock of laying hens and the gardens, tending the lobster traps and the increasing demand for air-sea rescue.

Ben remarked to Rose, that she was doing too much for them, but Rose was in her element, to her work came easily. She felt alive again now that she was contributing as she used to at Sweetwater Farm. She was getting used to her so-called retirement, but had left a lot behind when she left the farm. Rose was thoughtful for a long moment, and she said to Ben, "There is an older man in town, who used to be on the farm, helping my Charlie and I. He is as bored with his life now as I used to be. His name is Arthur Lister and he has been in here to buy eggs." Ben remembered him.

Rose continued, "I know he and his wife are having hard times making ends meet. I will speak to him, if you wish me to, and ask him if he would like to help us out. He knows the farming business inside out, and he'll never let you down."

Arthur Lister started helping Ben and Sarah the following Monday. He was pleased to be able to be back, helping produce crops.

Rose insisted that he be paid above the going rate. "If

you want good to help you have to pay them well, and make them feel they are as valuable in the world as you are."

Arthur took a lot of the workload off Ben, Sarah and Rose. What had begun as a family small garden was now a full time business.

One day Ben had a visit from a man from the 'Ministry of Food.' Rationing of food was getting tighter by the day. He came and told Ben he could no longer sell eggs to his customers. Ben and Sarah were getting quite upset. They were only 14 but had developed an independence for producing and selling to anyone they wished. The stranger looked at Ben, quite understanding his attitude. He had dealt with farmers and egg producers, and knew how independent they could be. He said to Ben, "I have heard about you. You're the young fellow who took his boat to Dunkirk. I have a boat too, and I also went over."

Ben was surprised, and immediately felt some affinity with the stranger.

The man explained to Ben and Sarah how the government, in order to make sure everyone had enough, must share equally all food produced, which included eggs.

"Otherwise we would have some people having plenty, whilst others will starve," he said. Ben countered, "My operation is so small. I wonder you would bother with it." The man replied that he would not be there if it was not important. "I expect you produce eggs for a good many people's rations," he said.

Sarah entered into the conversation; "What do you want us to do?" she asked. "I want you to pack all the eggs and ship them to the depot that has just been set up. Your eggs will be picked up and paid for every week. There is another thing I expect you already know some of your customers are buying your eggs and re-selling them at a huge profit."

Ben and Sarah then understood. The man continued, "Any reject or cracked eggs you can sell, but not all to one customer. Everyone must share." So Ben and Sarah registered as egg producers. The man left saying, "You will be paid a fair and good price – and please produce as many egg as you can." He also purchased some vegetables and then left.

Ben and Sarah had work to do sorting out vegetables in the shed at the end of the barn. Arthur and Rose were busy in the field 'cutting cabbages'.

Ben and Sarah worked in silence for a while. Sarah stopped what she was doing and said to Ben, "We have something we must talk about! When you kissed me 'goodnight' last evening – I felt a feeling I never had before." Sarah knew she was clumsy with words but continued, "If things go any further between us, and get out of hand…" She stopped, looked at Ben and expected him to say something. Ben said he too knew they were no longer just friends, saying, "I wonder what will happen to us." She said, "I suppose we will get married one day." Ben asked her if that was a proposal – to which they both laughed.

Sarah now said, "We can not make love until we are both at least sixteen." Ben replied, "No one will find out." Sarah said, "If I get pregnant our world, as we know it, will end – and you could go to prison." Ben said, "It will be a year and a half until we are sixteen." Sarah agreed and replied, "I hope this doesn't mean you will find another girlfriend." Ben moved across between the space between them. He held her close for a while and said, "You are the only girl I ever want," and added, "never will I want another girl." They agreed not to do anything to provoke each other that way. They both knew what they wanted but couldn't have: 'the forbidden fruit.'

The Battle of Britain was raging to its most intensive state. Planes were crashing in the channel, and the air-sea rescuers saved all they could, never getting used to pulling dead airmen from the water. But the Dunkirk rescuers became expert at what they were doing and rescued far more men alive than the few that had died. They rescued Germans as well as British airmen.

The coast guard had set up their station on the cliff overlooking the harbour. They were often alerted to aircrew in difficulty and the rescue boat crew were quickly informed before the plane crashed. The air-sea rescue boat would be at sea before the aircrew parachuted down.

Hitler was sure he could beat the RAF. His airforce had swept the sky of all opposition in the countries he had attacked so far.

The Bennett family were still worried that Britain would be beaten. They dreaded their fate should the Germans invade. Reports were getting out of Germany and countries the Germans had occupied, of Jewish people being rounded up and sent to death camps. The Bennett's could not understand the British; the more they were hurt, the more they fought back. Despite Dunkirk, no one questioned who would win the war amongst the general British population.

Each morning the BBC broadcast the losses of every side from that day. The RAF pilots fought day after day over southern England – over their heads.

The Germans, when rescued from the sea, were made prisoner of war. RAF pilots were put back into the battle, and fought on.

Every day from mid-August to mid-September the *Syrup of Figs II* put to sea to save pilots and aircrew.

The two-way radio was buzzing; a few times they switched onto the radio frequency of the aircraft and directed the aircraft and pilot towards the rescue boat.

Rarely, Sarah spoke to the German pilots in fluent German. She always told them she was Jewish, and they could tell their people that they had been saved by a Jew. Always, when they hauled a German from the sea, she would look at them, all subdued and soaking wet, and wonder why they were rounding up her people and murdering them. She could not understand the British either; fighting for their very existence, shooting Germans down, trying to kill them, and then going to great lengths to save them from the sea.

Everyone knew Britain was alone. The Americans, who could have helped, didn't. The Russians seemed to be on the Germans side, which only left Britain and the Empire alone, standing for all that was decent, against the monsters of Europe, and their Italian friends.

The days went by. The battle for the mastery of the air was getting worse, the most difficult day being 15th September 1940. The Germans threw all the planes they could, on that day, into battle. More aircrew were rescued on that day than any other. The *Syrup of Figs II* was busy all day. In the afternoon *Syrup of Figs I* was pressed into service. Ben and Sarah took her out to pick up two pilots – one of which had been badly injured but hopefully would survive. That evening the BBC broadcast at 9:00 p.m. One hundred and eighty-four German planes had been shot down. There were lesser air battles to come, but the RAF had won the 'Battle of Britain.'

Ben and Sarah were tired of being at sea all that day when requested to do so. They heard the news, and Ben walked home with Sarah. They hugged each other. Ben kissed Sarah 'goodnight' and walked on home.

Rose was at the Carter home, having a light supper. She said she had been so worried about Ben and Sarah at sea that day. She said with a small smile, "At least he hasn't gone to Dunkirk again." There was a knock on the door, no one usually came calling that late, it was the Bennett family.

Sarah looked at Ben and smiled – a gesture not unnoticed by grandmother Rose. With the wisdom of her age, she saw exactly what was there – deep affection. Mr Bennett spoke first, apologising for coming so late. There had been a letter smuggled out by a cousin in Germany. Many Jews had been rounded up including David Bennett's family and friends. David said, "If we had stayed in Germany, we would have been taken too. We are so grateful at being accepted in England, but we are very worried that Germany will invade England. If Hitler decided to invade England, our fate would be disastrous." There was silence. Tom asked David if he had heard the 9 o'clock news.

"No!" said David. He continued, "I've been afraid at what I might hear." Tom Carter repeated what the broadcast had said. "The RAF shot sown 184 planes today, they have won the 'Battle of Britain.' The German army can't cross the English Channel unless the German airforce could have defeated the RAF. The Germans haven't done so. The British Home Fleet is intact. With air cover, the Navy could reek havoc on the Germans.

Since Dunkirk, the army has grown stronger by the day. We now have a good Home Guard. People might say, 'What good will the Home guard be?' While a lot of them are veterans of the 1914-18 War I am pretty sure, in fact very sure, that Hitler could not invade England, even if his army was ten times the size," he said.

Tom continued, "Many people, over the centuries, have forecast England's 'doom.' With no exception, they have always been proved wrong. The Germans will lose the war. They lost it at Dunkirk. We will have some supper and, when you go home, have a good night's sleep. We are in for hard and difficult times but we will win. I am so sorry your family and friends in Germany have been taken – but we are very pleased you came here."

Ben had never heard his father speak to anyone so forcefully. He felt reassured too – as well as the Bennett's.

The Bennett's left for home, less nervous than when they had come. Ruth remarked, "How lucky we were to get to England when we did." They still couldn't quite understand the British – no country in the world could fight on the face of such power as was in Germany. Britain was alone but getting stronger by the day. The RAF had bombed Berlin.

David Bennett had made a new uniform for Sarah – it didn't help to win the war but it certainly looked better than the one she had been issued with.

The Bennett's had prospered in their tailor business. They were able to take advantage of the large amount of materials they had purchased before they left Germany, that had been delivered to Uncle David, in London. So much had happened since their departure from Germany.

Rebecca – who had escaped with them, had been promoted in her job at the Red Cross. She had an advantage of being fluent in German and English and had been asked by the Red Cross in Switzerland names etc. of German aircrew who had been either killed or captured in the 'Battle of Britain'. There was irony in being about to report German losses – and compensated somewhat for the news she was hearing of the losses inflicted by the Germans on her people in Germany.

The Germans switched their airforce to night bombing. Their decision, they were sure, would force Britain to surrender. London took a terrible beating. Every major town was blitzed, towns were bombed, and every village was attacked. Britain would not give in. They became more determined than ever to win the war.

Mussolini, the Italian dictator, whose ego knew no

bounds, was intent on invading Egypt. His army suffered a terrible defeat.

The first good news of the war was that the British destroyed an Italian fleet, a very powerful force destroyed or put out of action. The Germans invaded the Balkan countries, but at least Britain had been able to reduce the threat of Italy's power.

Ben and Sarah had fewer trips out with the air-sea rescue now that the 'Battle of Britain' was over. There were not as many aircrew to rescue.

Ben and Sarah worked hard, growing and selling their produce. Arthur Lister came to work one day, and couldn't stop smiling. He was so happy about something. Ben couldn't resist asking him what was so funny. Arthur replied, "It wasn't really funny." but he and his wife, with their extra income from Ben, had purchased a new wireless. He had never been able to afford one before, and said; "Now we can keep up with the rest of the world."

Ben and Sarah were issued with a permit to take the *Syrup of Figs* out fishing, which was necessary now in a wartime situation. They continued harvesting lobster, selling fish and lobster to a ready market.

The harbour had been fortified in case the Germans invaded. It was no longer the peaceful place it used to be.

Mr Brooks continued to tutor Ben and Sarah – they were easy to teach and learned readily. Mr Brooks was able to keep their interest. He then had an idea. He had dealt quite successfully with buying and selling shares on the stock market. What better way to teach Ben and Sarah mathematics? He asked Ben and Sarah if they were interested in investing money in stocks and shares. Mr Brooks explained how it was done. He suggested they invested £100 and get to understand the business by partaking in it.

Ben and Sarah were enthusiastic and readily agreed.

The next time they went to Mr Brooks for lessons they brought with them £200. They spent all evening discussing where they would invest it. Sarah wanted to invest in something solid and secure. Ben, a bit of a gambler, wanted to put the money into less secure places, with a chance of the shares going up fast.

Mr Brooks' idea was a good one and a compromise was arrived at. £100 Sarah's way and the other £100 Ben's way.

Every week they discussed their investment, sometimes they would sell shares, and re-invest in other shares.

Ben and Sarah began coming in for a cup of tea every morning from their work into the Carter home. They would grab the daily paper, turn to the financial pages, and discuss between themselves how things were going.

Tom and Ellen, although surprised at Ben and Sarah coming in every morning, didn't realise why.

The miserable winter of 1941 seemed to last forever. With rain and fog, trips to the sea were fewer, but not much good news had been reported. The U-Boats were sinking ships at sea, the bombing continued through the winter, until late spring and then almost stopped. Britain could not be beaten that way. The Germans had killed many thousands of civilians – destroyed whole cities – but Britain, the Commonwealth and the Empire fought on.

In early June, the BBC broadcast that the Germans had attacked The Soviet Union. Britain was alone no more. At first the Germans advanced into the Soviet Union toward the outskirts of Moscow, and though the Soviet Union losses were enormous, with the help of the winter the Germans were halted.

The RAF continued to bomb Germany and were now handing back to Germany what they had done to Britain.

The Germans had joined with the Italians in North

Africa, and had success against Britain and the Commonwealth forces. On the 7th of December 1941, Japan bombed Pearl Harbour.

Hitler then declared war on America. The British people, although prepared to fight on, no matter what, were relieved and pleased that the Americans were at last fighting in the war.

The British had known they would win the war – now they were doubly sure.

Ben and Sarah had expanded their operation and now had cultivated every part of the field, with the chicken wire runs also taking up some of the land.

Ben had asked several local farmers if they would sell him some of their grain to feed his chickens, but with no success, until a local farmer came to Ben and asked him to help with the threshing. The threshing contractor took his equipment from farm-to-farm – threshing the year's harvest for the farmers in the area.

He didn't have enough crew to operate it. The prospect of working for someone else did not appeal to Ben.

A tractor drove the threshing machine with a long belt attached from the tractor to the thresher. Ben thought for a while, after having refused the farmer, then he had an idea. The farmer was about the leave Ben's field, where they were talking. He was surprised how good and neat Ben's crops were looking and said so to Ben and Sarah. He told them he had grown crops all his life – but had never seen any better than theirs. Ben and Sarah were very pleased to hear the good comments. Ben asked that if he agreed to help with the farmer threshing could he be paid for his labour with grain instead of cash. The farmer thought for a while and then said, "Can you bring your tractor and trailer if you can come over." Arthur Lister was with them, and he knew the farmer, a Mr Wright, a bit on the mean side, but always fair. Arthur said, "Excuse me, but if Ben and Sarah are agreeable, I could help. I can drive the tractor over, as Ben has no licence to travel on the road." Mr Wright agreed, and asked Ben why he needed the grain and how much he needed? Ben repeated he would take grain instead of wages, and would also purchase some at the going rate. He said he wanted about two tons, and could he buy some beans too from the thresher. They agreed a price to be paid in cash. Ben added that it would feed his flock of hens. Sarah agreed reluctantly to stay at home on the farm.

Threshing started on Monday, as planned. The abundant crop yielded well. The Ministry of Food took the wheat quickly away by trucks to be made into flour and then into bread – which was in great demand.

Ben and Arthur tended the bags of grain as they were being filled from the thresher – loading them onto Ben's trailer and taking them to the granary. The days passed quickly. The work was hard for everyone involved. Mr Wright worked as hard as anyone, besides supervising the operation.

Ben and Arthur returned home every night with sacks of grain, barley, oats and beans, enough for him to expand his flock of hens.

Sarah was quite unhappy at Ben going away – they had always been together except when Ben went to Dunkirk. She was very pleased when Ben's stint at threshing was over.

Arthur enjoyed the experience – he said it was just like the old days. He felt he was living again, and not restricted to his house in town, with nothing of interest to occupy his time.

Ben and Sarah continued their education with Mr Brooks. They had more time with him, as the air-sea rescue was less demanding.

Mr Brooks told them there was a new headmaster at

Ben's old school. He said the new headmaster wanted to meet both Ben and Sarah. Mr Brooks had told him that he was tutoring two former students of the school, and why they had left. Ben's attitude hardened immediately, "If he is going to try to persuade me to go back to that place," he said emphatically, "Sarah and I will not go back to school. I never what to meet another schoolteacher."

Mr Brooks was surprised at Ben's anger, but added, "He wants to find out who the bullies at school are, so that he can protect the younger pupils. He is already aware of the failings of some of the teachers in dealing with the bullies."

Ben apologised for his anger and said again, "I will not go back to school." Ben and Sarah continued their lessons with Mr Brooks.

On the way home, Sarah said, "Ben – I have never seen you so cross. I think if you see the new headmaster you should talk to him, for the sake of the children, like you, who were bullied so badly, and whose actions were condoned and never stopped by Miss Taylor and her colleagues."

Ben did not reply – but Sarah was right. The new headmaster did drop by when Ben and Sarah were in their field working. He stopped at the gateway where Miss Taylor had entered the field and had got herself into trouble with her dog.

Ben and Sarah walked over and spoke to him. He introduced himself as Richard Morton. Mr Brooks had forewarned him that Ben did not like schoolteachers. Mr Morton gradually brought the conversation around to the reason for his visit. He said he was in charge of the school and wanted to know who the bullies were. Ben refused, "Your teachers know who the bullies are!" Mr Morton tried a new tact and said, "If you were just starting school – would you tell the situation to the teachers?" Ben said,

"No, if I complained to Miss Taylor she would call me a buffoon in front of the whole class." Mr Morton could see Ben was getting upset. He thanked Ben for talking to him, and complimented them on their huge garden.

He told them how fortunate they were to be tutored by Mr Brooks. With one last try, he said, "Just tell me two of the worse bullies." Ben gave in and said, "Bakely and Tarshall."

Mr Morton said he was sorry to hear that – they are now both prefects. Mr Morton left – wishing them a good day, and thanking them for their time. He walked thoughtfully back to his school.

The first thing he did upon his return, was to ask for Miss Taylor to come to his study. He didn't like the woman but he was responsible for his teachers. He said, "I understand there is a lot of bullying going on at the school, do you know anyone who is bullying another less fortunate? Do you ridicule your pupils in any way in class?" She lied easily – and said, "No – I wouldn't do such a thing."

Mr Morton continued, "Have you seen the two new prefects, Bakely and Tarshall, bully the children?" Miss Taylor again lied, "No!"

Mr Morton addressed her. "Miss Taylor, I have, on good authority, heard you have deeply insulted some of your pupils, and you are responsible for pupils leaving the school. If you ever do it again you will be dismissed, and I will not give you any reference whatever."

Miss Taylor left the headmaster's study, her arrogance quite deflated.

Mr Morton sent for Bakely and Tarshall and, when they arrived in his study, he got straight to the point. They had swaggered into his study – thinking they must be doing a good job as prefects for the headmaster to send for them. Mr Morton looked at them up and down – he didn't like them, anymore than he liked Miss Taylor. "There has been a complaint of your bullying of small pupils." They both denied any such thing. Then Mr Morton said, "You lie as well. Hand over your prefect badges, you will never bully anyone again – or you will be expelled from the school." Most of the bullying at school ceased.

The United States Airforce began arriving in Britain in early 1942. The American planes were easily recognised by the stars on their wings and sides. American soldiers began arriving in Britain. The losses to shipping in 1942 were enormous. Food rationing again tightened to include all the commodities that weren't before rationed.

The Battle of Stalingrad took place in the winter of 1942/43. The Germans lost, the Battle of El Alemein was about to begin and British and Commonwealth armies were about to attack the Germans and Italians.

The Bennett's were invited to supper at the Carter home. Tom asked if they were now more confident about the outcome of the war. They smiled, and said they were. Ben and Sarah were, as usual, together. Sarah complained she didn't feel well. She had been in pain for a couple of days, but thought she would be all right. Ben was anxious about her condition and eventually persuaded her to see the doctor.

The doctor examined her and asked her several questions. Sarah said, "The pain has gone now – I knew it would be all right." Instead of explaining anything to Sarah and Ben the doctor picked up the telephone and called the local hospital. He ordered the operation room to be readied for an appendectomy. He drove Sarah to the hospital in his car. Ben came too – bewildered by the turn of events. The doctor went into action immediately. Sarah had a ruptured appendix, which was very serious. He explained to Ben. Ben asked if Sarah would soon recover, the reply stunned

Ben. The doctor said, "I have done all I can do, she should have been operated on at least three days ago."

Sarah, his Sarah, was gravely ill. Thoughts of doom raced through Ben's mind. All the thoughts ended the same way without Sarah there was nothing.

Ben waited at the hospital for Sarah to come round from the anaesthetic. It seemed like an eternity but, only just over two hours later, Ben was taken in to see her. Sarah's parents, who had been informed right away, were the first to go in and see her, then Ben. Sarah opened her eyes, and smiled weakly at Ben. She was desperately ill. The burst appendix was taking its toll. Sarah went back to sleep, and Ben waited at the hospital. He felt helpless, and didn't know what to do. There was nothing he could do but wait.

The doctor came to see Sarah several times. Ben asked him how she was, to which he replied, "Sarah is gravely ill." Ben asked, "Do people usually recover from a burst appendix?" The doctor replied, "Some do, but I have never seen one as bad as she has now. I have placed a tube in the area of the poison to drain it. I have done all I can do – but we must not give up. I have seen strange things happen since becoming a doctor. Sometimes people who are desperately ill will recover. Others, who are not so ill, do not. I think you should go home Ben, you need some rest." Ben refused, as the doctor had expected. The doctor knew them well, and that they were always together.

Tom and Ellen came early to the hospital to see Sarah. They thought the world of her. The doctor told Tom and Ellen how very ill Sarah was. Tom asked, "Will she make it doctor?" The doctor replied, "I don't expect her to. I have seen this happen before. There is though, one small ray of hope – after I have cleared up the mess of the burst appendix with the new drug sulphanilamide. It might help. Try and persuade Ben to go home with you for a rest. I think his heart is broken. Take him to see his grandmother; she will understand better than anyone how to help Ben. She has been through it herself when Charlie died." The doctor then said he would go and see Rose and prepare her for the worst.

Tom sat with Ben at the hospital and tried to talk about anything to take Ben's mind off his terrible ordeal. He even mentioned Ben going to Dunkirk – but it was of no use. He knew if Sarah died then Ben's life would end, not to die, but if Sarah was not longer with Ben, there was nothing on earth that would take her place. Tom had never known or heard of a bond so strong as Ben and Sarah had between them. Tom eventually persuaded Ben to come home. He told Ben his grandmother wanted him to be with her for a while.

In the early hours of the day, Ben went to see Sarah before going home. He spoke gently to her, held her hand briefly and left. She was sleeping, she didn't know that Ben had been there.

Rose was waiting for them to return from hospital and Ellen, who was very distressed, was there too. Rose was at her best, and took charge of the situation. She had lost her Charlie, as she called him. She knew Ben's grief and understood. With gentleness she spoke to Ben. She asked how Sarah was. Ben replied, "She was asleep." He couldn't add more. Tom answered for him – "The doctors and nurses are doing all that can be done. The doctor called a specialist in London, and there is a new drug called an antibiotic, which they may be able to get for Sarah. "If they are successful in getting it, he will call and a packet will be sent by train. I will pick it up from the station – and hopefully it will help Sarah."

The doctor arrived at the house, and Rose let him in, fearing the worst. The doctor said, "The new drug has been put on the train, and will be at the station in an hour. We will leave now." Then he spoke to Tom, "I will come with you in case of any difficulty." The road was empty of vehicles. There was a slight hold–up at the station where an army sentry asked to see their identity cards.

The doctor said there was an emergency, went through and picked up the parcel from his colleague in London, hoping the journey was not in vain.

Sarah's condition had not changed. The doctor read the instructions. He decided to use a drip to put the drug to use straight away. He placed it in Sarah's arm. There was no response to the needle prick. She was desperately ill. The doctor and Tom watched, for almost an hour, the steady drip entering Sarah's vein.

Tom wondered how such a small amount of liquid could conquer such a poison as that which was killing Sarah. Tom and the doctor left for their homes. Tom went to Rose's home. Ben was asleep. Rose had given him warm milk and honey, and had added a little Scotch whisky. Ben had drunk it and seemed to like it. Shortly after he had fallen to sleep.

The morning came and again Rose gave him warm milk, honey and whisky and he again dropped off to sleep.

Rose turned to Tom and said, "I don't think there is anything better – they gave it to me when my Charlie passed away."

Ben awoke in the afternoon, Rose replied to Ben's question of, "How's Sarah?"

"We are going to walk to the hospital now – It will do both of us good to have some fresh air." The doctor met them at the hospital outside Sarah's room.

Ben immediately asked, "How is she?" Ben never forgot the reply, "I think she is a little better. Her temperature has gone down a little, but she is still a very sick girl."

Rose and Ben went into Sarah's room. The doctor had

replaced the drip with a second one. The new drip dripped steadily into Sarah's arm. Rose quietly left, leaving the two together. Ben took Sarah's hand and tears rolled down his cheeks. Sarah opened her eyes briefly and smiled slightly. Ben said, "Please don't leave me Sarah." Whether she heard him, he didn't know. Ben looked at Sarah. He remembered the first time he had seen her; he remembered the rose he had given her when they were nine years old. They had been together ever since. He remembered Sarah crying on the wharf when he left for Dunkirk. He had a treasure of memories, which would always be with him.

Rose came back into the room – she took Ben's arm, and said they had to go.

On the way home Rose said to Ben, "Sarah will be all right. There are things we have to do in the garden and then we will walk back to see her in the evening.

Arthur had been busy in the garden and they joined him. He enquired how Sarah was – and was glad to hear that there was a slight improvement in her health. They told Arthur they would be going back to the hospital in the evening. Arthur said quietly, "I wish I could see her." The old man referred to Sarah sometimes as his princess – and he missed her.

Tom and Ellen had visited Sarah during the afternoon, their concern was evident, and the Bennett's arrived soon after. They were all encouraged by a nurse who told them that there was a slight improvement in Sarah's condition.

In the evening, Rose, Ben and Arthur walked to the hospital. Arthur had put on his best clothes in order to "look proper," as he said. They quietly entered Sarah's room. Ben again held Sarah's hand. She opened her eyes at his touch, and smiled up at him. Ben was overjoyed with relief. She turned her eyes toward Rose and Arthur. She looked at them for a few seconds then, realising who they were, smiled again.

After they left hospital Arthur said, "That was the sweetest smile I ever saw."

Walter Tuck came to Rose's home to enquire how Sarah was. He told her he had pulled up and re-baited Ben's lobster traps. He had steamed them and taken them to the shop, which Ben normally supplied. Ben thanked him. Walter told Ben that they were managing the air-sea rescue. There was not the demand for their services like there was during the 'Battle of Britain.'

Sarah steadily grew stronger and Ben called at the hospital to see her whenever he could. David and Ruth Bennett walked with him sometimes and closed their shop temporarily.

After eight days, Sarah sat up in bed for the first time. Ben was so relieved, and happy since the ordeal first began. The Bennett's and Ben walked home together. When they were abreast of the church, the bells began to ring out. They stopped walking, as did everyone else in the street.

The bells had been silent for over three years – only to be used to warn of an invasion. Someone remarked that the king had ordered the bells to be rung to celebrate the great victory of El Alemein. The British and Commonwealth army had defeated the German army – and the Italians

The eight bells in the church tower never sounded so grand.

David and Ruth walked with Ben to his home. The Carter's were standing outside their shop. Rose and Arthur were with them – listening to the church bells ring out over the town and countryside.

Sarah was getting well and on the road to recovery. They were all very pleased with Ben's news of her. Tom turned to the Bennett's and said, "I told you Britain would win. We are now well on the way to that goal. The RAF are bombing Germany at night, the Americans – by day.

The air-sea rescue was increasingly busy and was being called up to rescue aircrew, American and British.

Ben had been out in the *Syrup of Fig I* tending his lobster traps; Sarah was not yet well enough to go out on to the wharf.

Ben was almost back at the wharf when he saw Walter Tuck running down the pier towards him. While Ben was tying up the boat, Walter asked him to come out on an air-sea rescue and try and pick up some Americans who were calling out for help. The volunteers had been instructed how to use their radios. They had used them with success – being able to talk to aircrew before they crashed into the sea.

Tom and Walter were aboard and started the *Syrup on Figs II* in a very short time. They travelled out between the piers, increasing to full speed very quickly and soon covered a couple of miles. The coast guard had informed them of an American Flying Fortress that would crash somewhere about seven or eight miles out. It had an engine on fire, and was coming down rapidly. Ben switched the wavelength to enable him to contact the Americans on the plane. The volunteers had all been instructed how to handle a larger plane, but so far they had never had to deal with one crashing.

Americans crews had been rescued from the sea before, individually. The pilot spoke first, asking if there was anyone down there to help. Ben replied, "Air-sea rescue at sea heading due south from Midhampton, England." Ben searched with his binoculars the sky – to the east – trying to locate the "Flying Fortress". The radio came to life; "Little ship – Can you see us – we are going north of you." Ben swung his gaze to the north – how had he missed it? Ben responded, "I have you in sight." Then the training they had received and put into operation came in very useful.

The American pilot said, "Can you see us?" Ben replied, "Yes, you are south of us, are you going to ditch or evacuate and parachute down?" The American replied, "We are going to attempt a landing." Ben said, "Will you raise your landing wheels?" If he had tried to land on water, they had been taught, with landing wheels down they would be in serious trouble.

Ben watched, through his binoculars, the wheels retract. Ben now said, "Can you cut your speed? You are at about 4,000 feet, and coming down too fast. Slow your speed, and keep the nose of the plane up." He continued, "You are still going too fast – slow your speed."

Ben opened the radio to the coast guard and said, "They have wounded on board – request doctor and ambulance."

Ben to plane: 'Will you move your wounded to the rear of the plane next to the exit? You must hurry – you are down to about 500 feet, slow your speed – keep your nose up. Just before you hit the water, cut engine at 40-foot altitude. We are travelling with you, and will be right there when you land. Have you any morphine?"

Pilot: "Yes!"

The pilot was getting testy. 'Who was down there giving orders?' After all, he was flying the plane.

Ben: "Have you moved your wounded? Time is running out."

The American replied, "Yes, sir!"

Ben said, "You are doing 100 mph – slow your plane – keep up the plane's nose – you are almost down."

The plane hit the water, slid along the surface and stopped. Walter and Ben were aside in a few moments. The wounded were taken off first – the others quickly followed. Walter and Ben moved the boat away from the rapidly sinking plane and headed for home.

The pilot asked where the 'admiral' was who was

giving the orders. Walter pointed to Ben. "But he's only a kid!" said the American. Walter retorted, "He got you down, didn't he?"

After a while, the pilot moved up beside Ben, who was at the wheel, and said, "Thank you." The *Syrup of Figs II* was living up to her name.

They went as fast as the boat had ever done. Despite the speed, the ride was fairly smooth. They either had to get to shore fast or take time and lose valuable time for the wounded.

The ambulances were waiting, as was the doctor. In no time at all the wounded were in hospital.

Rescuing Americans happened several times for the volunteers in the air-sea rescue from Midhampton.

The next American 'mayday' was an American out of fuel. It was one of the easiest rescues they made. Ben and Walter were on the scene quickly, and the plane sank unusually slowly.

Sarah continued to recover. She left the hospital, spent some time at home, and then she came and sat in the garden where she loved to be.

When Ben and Arthur took a break from their work they would sit with her, and enjoy tea from a flask they nearly always had at hand.

Ben and Sarah's life gradually returned to normal, at least, as normal as could be, allowing for the war. Their visits to Mr Brooks resumed. The investments Mr Brooks had handled for them were doing well. They had more than doubled their value – some doing better than others. They were learning faster than Mr Brooks had expected.

Ben and Sarah had been discussing investing more money. Their savings had grown dramatically.

Rose made sure Arthur Lister was well paid. Mr Brooks reluctantly agreed to invest £500 into a low priced stock. Rose had lectured Ben many times; "You cannot get good help without paying good wages."

Arthur and his wife were quite well off, compared to life before Arthur came to help Ben and Sarah – and Rose, of course.

Ben and Sarah tried to get Rose to accept something for the help she had given them. She became so indignant and upset that Ben never mentioned it again.

Rose and Arthur gave Ben and Sarah something they didn't realise they were giving – a wealth of knowledge, gathered over a lifetime.

Ben and Sarah continued to come in for morning tea or coffee at the Carter home. They immediately read the daily paper. The most interesting page was the financial page, as usual.

Ellen was beginning to wonder why, one morning, Ben and Sarah became very excited. The new stock they had purchased had doubled. Mr Brooks would be pleased. Ellen asked what they were so excited about. Ben replied, "We saw something in the paper." They were sitting at the kitchen table, the financial page laid open. Ellen said to Ben, "How can a financial page be so exciting unless…" She stopped, and then continued, "You haven't been investing money have you?" Sarah couldn't hold out any longer saying, "The stock which we have just purchased has more than doubled." Ellen had mixed feelings: pleasure, pride, and some fear. "How did you start investing – and when?" she asked. They told her the whole story.

It was Mr Brooks' way of getting them interested in maths. Ellen asked, "How much have you invested?" Ben said, "As of now about £1,500 and quickly added, "we must quickly go back to the garden – we have a lot to do."

Ellen went next door to see Rose, blurting out, "Did you know Ben and Sarah have been investing in the stock market?" Rose replied, "Yes!" Ellen said, "Why didn't you let us know?" Rose replied, "It is their money. It was none of my business really." Ellen then said to Rose, "They may have lost it all." Rose told Ellen that Mr Brooks was helping them, and he is successful with his investments. Rose had no fear of them losing their money, and added, "Remember they work hard for the reward the receive, and how they spend it is their affair. Remember when Ben wanted to buy the field and you were against that too?"

Rose was now 'getting in gear' as they say. "If Ben and Sarah want to do something like this, I am right behind them. Ben is going a long way with his life – so don't interfere."

Ellen had received lectures from mother Rose before, but not lately. She quickly backed away from the subject.

She would tell Tom though. He would have something to say – but Rose was there first. Ellen had left the shop to do some shopping in the town. Rose went to the chemist shop and asked if her daughter was home. Tom said that she had just left to do some shopping in town. Rose said, "Oh!" and was about to leave, but stopped at the door and asked Tom innocently if he knew that Ben and Sarah dealt in stocks and shares. Tom was making up a prescription, half-listening to his mother-in-law, and said, "Nothing would surprise me about those two." Tom stopped what he was doing and said, "What did you say?" Rose repeated, "Ben and Sarah are investing in the stock market." Tom's first reaction was, "I will have to put a stop to that." He noticed Rose stiffen her back. She seemed to grow six inches when provoked, saying, "You will do no such thing." Rose explained how it all started, "Mr Brooks thought it was a good way to help teach maths. He is quite successful with his investments. When Mr Brook complains to you, then give Ben and Sarah some advice – but not before. It is their money, which they have worked hard for, not yours." Rose was about to add more, when Tom said, "All right," and burst out laughing. He then said to Rose, "What will those two do next? They own a field, their have a good business, and they are not yet sixteen years old." Rose left the shop.

Ellen returned a while later from shopping. Straight away she told her husband about Ben and Sarah investing in the stock market. Tom said, "I know all about it. Your mother told me." No more was said.

Mr Brooks was very pleased their investment was doing well, but still had some misgivings about it. He advised waiting a while, and trying to sell at the right time. In a few weeks the stock had doubled again. Mr Brooks advised them to sell. Their initial investment of £500 was sold for £4,000. They then invested in several different stocks and shares. Even a small increase in the value now made a difference. They were receiving dividends. Their maths lesson, to Mr Brooks pleasure, was paying off.

Ben and Sarah continued to help Mr Brooks with his garden. Most of the time they would discuss many subjects as they worked. Sometimes Mr Brooks would draw something significant, or a map, in the freshly tilled earth, to explain something, or in order to make a point. He received a steady supply of lobster, fish plus eggs, which were all in short supply elsewhere. So he was very pleased with the arrangement he had made with them, i.e. the payment.

Sarah, Arthur and Ben were working in the field, cutting cabbages and bagging them for the market. The crop was good. The chickens provided the fertiliser for the needs of the huge garden. Other crops were also looking good.

Sarah had completely recovered from the ordeal that had almost cost her her life.

Arthur was quiet as though something was on his

mind. Usually he talked more than he did today. Ben eventually said to him, "There's something bothering you, isn't there Arthur?" He hung his head a little and said, "Yes, there is, there is something the wife wants me to ask you…!" He hesitated… "Could you take the wife and I out to sea when you go out to the lobster traps?" Ben and Sarah stopped work and asked, "Why do you what to go?" Arthur replied, "It doesn't matter. I should not have asked – but neither of us has ever been out to sea." Ben and Sarah said they would be delighted to have them come onboard. It would give them a lot of pleasure to take them.

Arthur said, "Can I leave work early today? It's a bit soon, but I must tell the wife." Then he asked, "When shall we be going?" Ben agreed with Sarah that Sunday would be a good day. Arthur left in a hurry to break the good news to his wife.

Rose appeared, coming down the centre of the field. She stopped occasionally to look at the crops growing in neat rows. She came over to Ben and Sarah and asked if Arthur was all right, as he was leaving early. "They are coming out with us when we tend the lobster traps on Sunday. In all their years living by the sea, they have never been out in a boat." Rose said quietly, "Neither have I. Charlie and I always promised each other that we would, but there was always something that prevented us from doing it."

Sarah realised that the old lady felt left out, and felt a bit hurt. She said, "Grandmother Rose – will you come with us? There is plenty of room on the *Syrup of Figs*."

Rose was delighted. The first thing she said was, "What shall I wear?" They laughed together. "It doesn't matter too much, we won't meet anyone," said Ben.

The following Sunday, as planned, they all met on the wharf. It was a late spring day. The sun was pleasantly warm and the sea was calm.

Mrs Lister wore her best clothes, usually reserved for church. Arthur wore a tie for the occasion and put on his best shirt. Ben had never seen Arthur wear a tie before. Ben and Sarah told them they would go up the coast, to where Ben had spent the night on his way home from Dunkirk.

Ben started the motor, cast off the ropes, and sailed out between the piers. A few people were watching them. Mrs Lister sat bolt upright, on one side of the boat, with Rose on the other. Rose said, "I used to come down here as a girl and watch the city gentry, on holiday, go out on their boats. How I use to envy them." Mrs Lister said she did exactly the same.

They turned east after leaving the harbour. Ben increased speed, and told them that the trip would take about one-and-half hours. They all enjoyed the trip. Ben spotted the small beach, reduced the speed and sailed into shore. The boat was pulled in far enough for the ladies to climb out without getting their feet wet.

Ben looked around. The log embedded in the shingle was still there. Memories came back to him of the last time he had been there, thoroughly exhausted.

Sarah asked Ben where he had slept that night on his way home. He replied, "By that old log." Rose joined in the conversation, "So this is where you spent your fourteen birthday! Next week you will be sixteen."

Ben looked at Sarah, she was blushing. She remembered the promise they had made to each other many months ago. She knew what would take place after their birthday. Neither could hold back any longer from really making love. Their lives together would be complete.

Mrs Lister asked Ben how far Dunkirk was from there. Ben replied, "About two hundred miles." She asked if Ben would do it again. Sarah answered for Ben. "No, he's never going to do any such thing again if I can prevent it." Ben took hold of both Sarah's hands She was getting upset at the memory of what had happened. He looked into her eyes, tears very close, and said, "No, I will never leave you again. Never."

They were all quiet for a while. They had witnessed something very special between Sarah and Ben. Meg, who was always with them, was very interested in the excellent food that was being brought forward from the boat, and she had her usual share.

They walked around the little beach. Rose asked Ben what it had been like here, all alone, that night. Ben replied, "I don't know – I slept for twelve hours. I remember feeling cold when I woke up though. If I hadn't woken up for another hour, I would have had to wait for the next high tide to take me out."

Ben and Sarah walked along the small beach. Behind a small outcrop of the cliff Ben kissed her. He held her close and said, "We will be sixteen next week." Sarah replied, "I have been waiting, for what seems like an eternity." She asked Ben if he was prepared so as he would not make her pregnant. Ben said he would take the necessary precautions. He had purchased condoms from his father's shop when his parents were out.

"I have them in the locker of the *Syrup of Figs*." Then he mischievously added, "I'll get one and we'll try one out." They both laughed. Sarah asked Ben what they looked like. Ben said, again in fun, "About two feet long and four inches across." Sarah looked at Ben in horror, and realised that he was joking. They walked back to the small party on the beach. The *Syrup of Figs* was pushed out to sea. Meg was the first to jump aboard. Then the ladies got in, and they were soon all heading out to sea – the same as Ben had done alone, almost two years before.

Arthur, his wife and Rose, were having the time of their lives. They had expected the picnic to last, perhaps, a little longer. The sea had remained calm, luckily. Ben headed for the corks floating above the lobster traps. The corks were visible a few hundred yards ahead. Ben slowed the boat and began to haul the traps. They had a fair catch of lobster. Arthur's wife commented, "The only lobsters I ever see are pink. These live ones are nearly black," adding, "we never had lobster before Ben gave us some. We never could afford such luxury. We couldn't afford a wireless before Arthur helped Ben in the garden. Thank you Ben!"

The traps were re-baited and put back into the sea. On the way towards home, Ben and Sarah spotted mackerel. They had hoped conditions would be right for them to appear. Ben pulled a box from the front of the boat. There were hand lines in it, with lures on each. Ben and Sarah handed one each to Arthur, his wife and Rose, and told them how to use them. Hardly had the lines entered the water, when Rose caught the first fish she had ever caught.

Arthur and his wife soon caught more mackerel. The fish were abundant. The three older people were as excited as youngsters, and very pleased with their catch. Ben and Sarah took the fish off the lines for them. Ben was reluctant to stop them from their fun of fishing. They were having such a good time. The fish were more abundant than Ben had ever known, and they soon caught enough. They packed up their lines and headed for the harbour. Upon arriving Walter Tuck came running along the wharf – exactly as he had done before. He shouted, "There is an American plane in trouble. The coast guard says they are going to bail out over the sea." Ben quickly said to Arthur, "Can you get the ladies to the wharf, and look after the catch?" Arthur agreed.

Ben and Sarah left the boat and hurried to the *Syrup of*

Figs II. Walter had started the motor by then and untied her. He operated the throttle as soon as they were on board and headed out to sea. What a change; from a pleasant day to turn suddenly back to war.

Ben spoke to the coast guard over the radio. He asked if they had the position of the plane and what kind of plane it was. The reply came back, "A Flying Fortress – off course, and out of fuel. They are heading your way – but are coming down." Ben searched towards the east with his binoculars, from side-to-side of the area he was viewing and said, "I can see them!" Then he tried to make radio contact, "American Fortress – can you hear me?" He repeated it after no response came. "Yes, I can hear you," the radio crackled as usual. "We have very little time – two engines have stopped and not working. We are losing height."

Ben: "Can you steer toward the west?"

Pilot: "Yes!"

Ben: "You will be over us in no time at all. Can you see us?"

Pilot: "Yes – have you in sight."

Ben: "Are you going to jump?"

Pilot: "Yes!"

Ben: "Will you try to jump as close together as possible. Make sure non-swimmers go first."

Pilot: "Will do! We are losing altitude fast – so have to evacuate plane now."

Ben: "Go ahead – we are ready." The stricken plane came over them. Men started falling from it. Ben asked them to get out quickly. The parachutes opened.

Sarah, now at the wheel, headed for an area she anticipated the aircrew would ditch in. Almost as soon as the aircrew landed at sea Ben and Walter pulled the first man aboard, the second and third men very quickly after. Walter and Ben had learnt early on that very sharp knives

117

were essential to cut parachutes off.

Within ten minutes of picking up the first airman they were all aboard the *Syrup of Figs II*.

Ben reported to the coast guard, "All have been rescued and are safely aboard." The coast guard acknowledged Ben's message then said there was another American in trouble somewhere near them. "He is in a bad way. He's flying a Mustang." All aboard heard the message. Ben started broadcasting right away, "Mustang, Mustang – can you hear me?" No reply. Ben tried again, "American Mustang – can you hear me?" Other than the crackle of the radio, nothing. Ben reached over in front of Sarah and stopped the motor. There was quiet. *The Syrup of Figs II* lay still in the water. Ben tried the radio again. "American Mustang – can you hear me?" he kept repeating. Then – an answer. "I hear you."

Ben: "Are you going to bail out or ditch?"

American: "I cannot bail out I am shot up too badly." Ben was again watchful and lucky. He spotted the plane.

Ben: "Can you see us, American?"

American: "No!"

Ben: "Can you manage to bring her down?"

American: "I think so."

Ben: "You are going to go down west of us."

Pilot: "Yes, I'll try."

Ben went through the same routine he had been taught, and had used before. "Cut speed – keep nose of plane up."

The pilot responded, "Okay!"

Ben: "Are you badly hurt?"

Pilot: "Yes!"

Ben: "Can you hold out a little longer?"

Pilot: "I'll try."

Ben: "You are at 1,000 feet and going too fast – cut speed but don't stall machine – keep nose of plane up."

Pilot: "Okay, I feel a little better now."

The *Syrup of Figs II* was racing at full speed below the plane but losing.

Ben: "Just before you ditch – cut your engine out."

Pilot: "Okay!"

The *Syrup of Figs II* was losing speed against the speed of the plane. A few seconds later the plane hit the water. The *Syrup of Figs II* raced for the downed plane at top speed trying to reach it before the plane sank into the water. Sarah was in charge of the wheel and, as they neared the plane, they could see no sign of life. Sarah took the boat over to the plane and kept the engine running just enough to keep the boat against the Mustang.

Walter and Ben jumped onto the wing of the plane. They had done this before. They carried short, but heavy, axes. Within a few seconds they broke through the canopy of the plane, pulled out their knives and cut the pilot free. They gently pulled the pilot out as fast as they could and handed him to the Americans that they had already rescued in the boat. They laid him in the middle of the *Syrup of Fig II*. The Mustang slid below the water. They had had no time to spare.

Ben went to the front of the boat. From a small compartment he removed a first aid kit. They had all been trained to administer morphine, which Ben proceeded to do, to deaden the pain the pilot was enduring.

They were already heading home when Ben called the coast guard, "Have Mustang pilot on board – needs immediate attention – are you ready?"

The coast guard, ambulance and doctor waited. The Americans on the *Syrup of Figs II* were more than impressed at the efficiency of the three who had rescued them, and the Mustang pilot. They had been saved by a couple of kids and Walter – one was a girl at that.

Sarah, still at the wheel, took the boat gently to a

standstill by the wharf. A stretcher was lowered and the wounded American was lifted on to the pier, into the ambulance, and off to hospital.

The sun had just set on a very eventful day, which had started so peacefully and then had been brought abruptly back to war. – The effect of which were never far away. The Americans were all grateful to Sarah, Ben and Walter. Some would not have survived without the air-sea rescue.

The small crowd, which had assembled, applauded the trio as they came on to the pier from the *Syrup of Figs II*.

Rose, Arthur, and his wife were still there to greet them. They had cleaned up the mackerel. Rose took the liberty of giving Arthur and his wife two dozen of the fish. They heartily thanked Ben and Sarah for taking them out to sea, and for the picnic. They were very pleased they were home from rescuing the airmen.

They all walked home together, all going to Grandmother Rose's home. They talked over the events of the day. Rose cooked mackerel for supper, that all present enjoyed.

Ben walked Sarah back to her home. She had brought fish for her parents. Ben held Sarah close when they embraced, before Ben left.

Sarah suggested they walk inland the following Sunday. It was someone else's turn to man the rescue boat. "We could go up the hill behind the farm, where Rose and your grandfather lived," she said. "Perhaps we could take a picnic and anything else that comes to mind," she added quickly.

The following week the garden was attended to. Vegetables were made ready to be sold. Two evenings Ben and Sarah went to Mr Brooks' house. The stock market was discussed. Mr Brooks suggested selling some shares and re-investing in others. Their investments were increasing in value, and with dividends their net worth, Mr Brooks estimated, to be close to £8,000.

Ben and Sarah were delighted. Mr Brooks was well pleased too, and teased them, saying: "You'll soon be able to retire."

The following Sunday Ben and Sarah left for their walk inland. It was a change from nearly always going to the sea, and the demands of the rescue boat. They didn't mind, and the countryside made a welcome change.

They walked steadily along the road from the town, passing Sweetwater Farm on their left, to the top of the hill, which was high enough to look down over the farm. The weather was kind, with sunshine. Various birds sang along the way. Sarah remarked, "I wonder if they are singing for us?"

They stopped at the gateway, giving them a better view of the farm, which Rose had described so often. They saw, on the right, the small woodland that Rose had also spoken of. It was in a small valley down the centre of which ran a stream, which carried the water from the springs from under the hill.

Rose had spoken of a small lake in the centre of the woods, made by the springs over the passage of time.

They decided to investigate. They walked across the fields to a stile at the edge of the woods. Beyond was a footpath, used very little, but still passable. This is how Rose had described the path that she and Charlie used to take to the small lake.

Ben and Sarah didn't have to walk very far through the tall ferns, and then, to their delight, the lake came into view. Large trees kept the lake a secluded place. Very few people knew of it and the purest water fed it. Ben remarked how the farm was named after this place 'Sweetwater Farm'.

The gentle breeze was not bothering the small lake. The surface was like a huge piece of glass. The birds sang amongst the trees, to be echoed through the area.

Ben and Sarah spoke of Rose and Charlie, Ben's grandparents, and wondered if they had come here when they were young. They were both warm, and Ben suggested they swim for a while.

Sarah said, "Well – we have no bathing costumes." Ben replied, "No one comes here – no one will see us." Sarah blushed as never before. She hesitated, and then started to unbutton her blouse. They undressed slowly. Each garment that was removed revealed parts of each other's bodies they had never seen before. They had known each other for seven years, and were closely held by an invisible bond that nothing would ever break, and yet, were unclothed before each other for the first time. They walked slowly into the water. To disturb such a place of utter peace seemed to them an intrusion. They swam together across the small lake. The water was slightly cool, but not at all unpleasant.

They returned to where they had entered the water. Neither would ever forget seeing each other's nakedness.

Ben thought, and was sure, that there was never a more beautiful sight than Sarah standing there at the water's edge and the reflection of her beauty in the now stilled water.

Sarah said to Ben, "Did you bring those things?" (meaning condoms). He said, "Yes. I didn't know whether to do so or not, but I hoped." He reached into his clothes and took out the small envelope holding one condom. Sarah took it and closely examined it. She unrolled it, and rolled it up again. She smiled and said to Ben, "It is not like you said – 'two feet long, and four inches wide'. I expect it will be just right." Sarah handed back the rubber to him, and sat down on the soft vegetation. Ben sat down

122

beside her, and pulled her gently down on her back. They made love for the first time.

They both lay back in the sun contentedly for a while, without speaking. Sarah moved first. She sat up and looked at her beloved, Ben. Although they were only sixteen years old, she knew their love would never waver. They had sealed their love in the peace of the Sweetwater springs.

Ben sat up and decided to eat what Sarah had packed.

"Food fit for a king," Ben said. They drank some spring water and were at peace with all things. They decided to go swimming again, and returned to their chosen spot.

Ben embraced Sarah and they made love again. They eventually decided it was time to go home. Ben commented, "We need to stay another half hour – there are ten more condoms to go." They both roared with laughter. They left anyway.

Walking back across the fields they took a different route from when they came, walking round to a track which took them to the farmhouse and buildings. Rose had, over the years, described the layout of the place.

The man who had purchased the farm when Ben's grandfather died came out to see them. They were, in fact, trespassing. Ben introduced himself and Sarah. He added, "She is my girlfriend." He had never used that term before. Ben explained that his grandfather used to farm Sweetwater Farm. The new owner was pleased to see them, and asked them into the house.

"My wife is away," he said. "She always wanted to live in the country. That is why I purchased the farm. She soon lost interest and prefers the city. I have not farmed the land like your grandparents did. It seems I pull one way and my wife another. A divided house cannot stand.

"Perhaps one day you will buy it back from me." He talked on. "When your grandmother left here, I met her just

123

as she was leaving. I have heard of people breaking their hearts. I will never forget how heartbroken your grandmother was. She and your grandfather, I have been told, were bound so close that, when he died, she almost died with him. When she could no longer run the farm and had to sell, it was a terrible blow, and one more heartbreak. I'll bet she is pleased to have a grandson."

Ben and Sarah said they would have to leave. They would be on call later that night for the air-sea rescue. Mr Fulton, the new owner, said, "I have heard about you both, and the good work you have done. I would like to see you living here one day. It would be good to see the farm pass back to your family."

They walked away from the farm, back towards home. They stopped at the farm entrance and looked back at the farm. Sarah said, "It is a beautiful place. Do you think we could really ever live there?" As they walked, they talked of the day's events. Sarah said, "I never imagined making love could be like it was." Ben said, "How do you mean?" Then Sarah replied, "It was a kind of pleasure I never expected. It seemed to seal our love."

Ben and Sarah returned to the Carter home. Tom and Ellen asked where they had been for their walk. They said, "North of Sweetwater Farm. We walked across the fields of the farm and we met the man who owns it." Neither Ben nor Sarah mentioned the woods or the lake. Ben said, "Mr Fulton, the new owner, may be selling soon."

Ellen said, "Don't tell your grandmother. She will start recalling her life there, and that always makes her unhappy." No more was said, except, they were pleased Ben and Sarah had had a nice day. "It's such a change for you to be away from the sea. You will probably remember it for a while."

Remember indeed. Ben and Sarah looked at each other

and smiled. Both thought to themselves they would never forget.

Ben and Sarah went to see Rose and walked around the crops in the field. The crops looked good. Ben had to go to the barn. It was getting dark. The day was almost over. They went to the area where grain was stored for the chickens. The inside of the barn was quiet and peaceful, as old barns often are. Ben and Sarah moved closer together. Ben held her close, then, without saying a word, he picked her up and placed her on the sacks of grain. They made love for the third time that day. Gently to start with and ending with the contentment only reserved for genuine lovers

Ben walked Sarah back to her home. When she had left home that morning she had been an innocent girl. She now knew about sex, and returned home that evening feeling fulfilled.

David and Ruth were worried because Sarah had been so late coming home. Sarah explained where they had been and that they had then checked the garden to see that all was well, and it was.

The flock of hens had increased. With Ben's help from threshing, he had a sure source of chicken feed, in exchange for working at the threshing machine. The chicken pens now took up two acres of the field they owned. The flock was divided into five equal pens, each holding two hundred chickens. A six-foot wire fence was erected to fence the chickens in. They had been on the same part of the field for nearly two years. Rose and Arthur, with a little diplomacy, told Ben and Sarah that it was time to move the pens. Ben asked why. "You are bound to get a build up of disease, keeping the birds in one place for too long." Ben and Sarah decided to buy new wire fencing, and stakes to put the wire on, and take up another two acres adjoining the pens now used.

Ben was able to purchase the materials required, despite wartime shortages. The old posts were placed neatly in a pile with the old wire fence. The new enclosures were erected on land previously used for various varieties of vegetables.

Ben used his tractor to cultivate the vacated chicken enclosures, which was easy after the chickens had moved to their new enclosures. The land worked well. It was very fertile an anything would grow there. The chickens had fertilised the area well and there were no weeds. The chickens had seen to that too and neither had any bug or beastie escaped their attention.

Ben and Sarah discussed what to grow. "The land will be bug free and weed free, so will not require any weeding," said Sarah. Ben put forward the idea of growing onions. He said the crop of onions they had grown the previous year had sold well, and they had made more money out of their onions than anything else.

Ben sent for the onion seed in due course. It was a rough guess, but he thought it was perhaps enough. There was an old seed drill with the tractor he had purchased. He never thought he would use it, but now it would be put into service.

The onion seed arrived in two packages. Ben harrowed the seedbed over once more, to help get the temperature of the soil up. He and Sarah sifted sawdust until it was roughly the size of the onion seed. He mixed the sawdust with the seed, to make sure the seeds were well spaced, to cut out the labour of thinning the seedlings. Arthur watched, quite speechless, casting a critical eye over the onion venture. This was the first time that he seemed to be apprehensive and disturbed by what was going on. They had taken his, and Rose's advice, by moving the chicken pens, but no one asked them anything about onions. Arthur asked, "What are you going to do with all those onions if they grow?" Sarah said, "Sell them!" The onions came up very quickly. The condition of the soil was perfect for growing onions, without Ben and Sarah realising it.

Grandmother Rose walked in the garden as she often did. None had mentioned to her what was planted there in the former chicken runs. She had not asked, but was curious. There were row upon row of green things about three inches high – neatly spaced. She wondered, and left. Later she saw Ben and Sarah. She asked, "What have you planted in the chicken field? Looks like onions, but I know it can't be" she said. Sarah said, "It is onions." Rose became a little testy and said "A joke is a joke, but what really IS growing out there?"

Ben answered her this time, "They really are onions. We did well selling them last year, and thought we would grow a few more." Rose said, "Few! Few! There's enough planted out there to feed half the Empire, and all of Britain too." She was a bit upset, and said to herself, 'Why didn't they ask me first?'

Arthur walked over to the onion field. He had a habit of pushing his cap up from the back of his head, which made the front come down a bit, over his nose. He too had an opinion. He said to Ben and Sarah, "Don't you think you have planted too many onions? Why not harrow some of the rows out? We will never harvest that lot. The only good thing I see, is the way they are growing. I have never, in all my days, seen onions grow like these are growing."

Word soon got out about the onion field. People came and asked permission to see the acres of onions.

Looking up the field all the rows were in perfect lines, dark green and making tremendous growth.

Every time a newcomer saw them the same question was asked, "What are you going to do with them all?"

After a couple of months, they had grown much faster than normal. The bulbs were already quite a size.

Arthur remarked, "They are bigger than any onions I have ever seen."

In late September Ben and Sarah pulled some of the onions and placed them in rows to dry. It was then that the quantity they had planted, made them realise, if they handled the crop themselves, they wouldn't finish harvesting them until after Christmas. They were worried about what to do.

Ben told his friend, Walter Tuck, about his dilemma. Walter said that his two boys might help. Walter asked, "What will the pay be?"

Ben was a little desperate about the crop. "We will pay four shillings an hour," which was twice as much as Walter was getting when he had worked for other people. Walter said, "I'm sure they will come. I expect my wife will come too," then he added, "dammit, I'll come as well for that pay."

The boys agreed to work from five to nine p.m. after school. That even speeded up production– but nowhere near that which was required.

Ben and Sarah were still worried. Arthur said, "I told you to harrow some out." Rose had nothing to say, which meant see didn't approve either.

That evening even Walter Tuck, his wife, and two sons arrived, plus a dozen boys and girls from their class at school. The first thing noticeable at school was the smell of onions. Walter's sons had on the same clothes at school that they had worn the previous evening pulling onions. They were teased.

One of Walter's sons said he didn't mind the smell Ben Carter was paying four shillings an hour. The teasing stopped abruptly. They asked if they could work and get four shillings an hour. The Tuck boys said they didn't know, but said, "Come round after school and see Ben and Sarah."

That was why there were twelve children out in the field, just standing and looking rather sheepish. One girl plucked up courage and went over to Ben and asked, "Please may we have a job pulling onions?" Ben replied, "Yes!" The girl said, "Do you really pay four shillings an hour?" Ben said, "Yes…but the work is hard." The other children joined in, and for four hours each night they worked, each taking home sixteen shillings, more than most of their parents earned.

There now arose a problem. Clothes were in short supply in wartime. They went to school in the clothes they had been wearing, with the same problem the Tuck boys had had. The classroom smelled of onions. The irony of it being that it was Miss Taylor's class. She asked why they smelt of onions. One pupil replied, "We worked for Ben Carter." Miss Taylor snapped, "You'll have to stop working for him." Another boy chirped up, "We can't do that Miss. The pay is four shillings an hour." She snapped back, "I don't believe you. That's more than I earn." The other onion pickers joined in, "Yes, we really do get four shillings an hour." Eventually Miss Taylor was convinced, saying, "I suppose we will have to put up with it." Then she had a thought. "All the onion pickers will change places with the pupils by the windows. And throw the windows open." It didn't help too much.

The Bennett's were working in their tailor's shop. Sarah came home for some reason. She was wearing her overalls and rubber boots. She kicked off her boots outside and walked into the house. She looked very pretty in overalls, as she did in anything else she wore. David got the first whiff of onions, as he worked behind the counter. "Where in Heaven's name is that smell of onions coming from?" he said. Sarah replied, "We have been harvesting onions." David snapped, "How on earth can I sell good clothes in a shop smelling of onions? Why is a pretty

Jewish girl having to pull up onions anyway? There is not even a mention of an onion in the Bible?" Sarah said she was sorry and left feeling hurt. She was crying. Ben had a similar experience as Sarah had. He kicked off his boots and walked into his house, taking with him the pungent smell of onions.

Tom said, "I have just received a shipment of toilet soap now it smells as if I sell onions." Ben left as Sarah had done.

Sarah went to see Rose. She was very upset as tears came easily to Sarah. She told Rose that Ben had the same treatment from his father. Now Rose was upset. Ben and Sarah had worked very hard harvesting their onions, whether it was a good idea or not. When Rose was angry she seemed to increase in stature. Tom and Ellen saw her come into the shop via the back way. Ellen said, "Mother is upset about something." Ellen knew the signs.

Rose came right into the shop and said, "What did you say to Ben to make him so upset?" Tom said, "He smelled so badly of onions – I asked him to go." Rose said, "You're never grown a damned onion in your life. He'll make more money from the onions than you'll make from this shop. Ben and Sarah need encouragement after all their effort with the onion field, as well as with other things. You will both of you leave things to me and don't say such hurtful things again." Rose walked out and slammed the door. She went back to her home, put on her hat and coat and went over to the Bennett's. Rose's hat, made her look even taller as, she sallied forth 'in full sail.'

Luckily there were no customers in it. David and Ruth were standing behind the counter. David said, "How can I help you Mrs Warton?" Rose replied, "Why did you find it necessary to bully Sarah a short while ago? She came to me very upset." David said, "I don't recall bullying her – but she stank of onions."

Rose continued, "People have been kind to you since you came here to live, and this is the way you behave towards your own family." Many had described Rose as a gentle lovable person, but don't ever cross her. Ruth asked Rose what was to be done about it. Rose said, "You will sell me another pair of overalls and clothes for her to change into when she leaves work for home." David said sheepishly, "We don't sell overalls." Rose said, "What kind of tailor shop is this. You don't sell overalls and you don't like onions. What is wrong with you?" Ruth ventured a suggestion. She would give Rose other clothes for Sarah to change into when she finished work. David said he would order some overalls in.

Rose took the clothes and walked out of the shop, giving the door a good swing as she departed. She smiled to herself, at her own sense of humour, as she walked home. It mattered not, whether Jew or Gentile – she had put up the 'fear of God up both.'

Rose walked to the onion field to see Ben and Sarah. "When you finish work, come in and change your clothes before you go home. No more will be said about it."

Ben, Sarah and Arthur used the wire from the old chicken pens to dry the onions. Wooden frames were made with the old posts, which held up the wire onto frames about two feet off the ground. The onions were spread on top of the wire to dry, which proved very efficient.

Soon the smell of onions wafted over the town. It proved to be an excellent way to advertise the crop. Onions were a scarce commodity in wartime. Soon a steady stream of people came buying them at a shilling-a-pound. An American Jeep pulled in. The soldiers onboard had traced the smell of onions to its source. They asked Sarah if the onions were for sale. Sarah asked, "How many would you want?" The American said, "There are three large army camps – and none of the cooks can buy good onions. Will you sell us fifteen tons?" Sarah didn't bat an eyelid, and said she would.

The Americans asked when they could pick up the onions and what price they were. Sarah said, "One hundred pounds a ton," and they could have five tons a day for the next three days, and perhaps they could have more later.

One American tried to ask Sarah for a date. She blushed and said, "No!" The American asked Sarah if the people who were working there were short of any item they might have to spare from their stores. Sarah said, "Pretty well everybody was short of jam."

Two elderly people came one day to the onion field. They stood for a while, watching the harvesting of the onions, but didn't move other than appearing to be interested. Ben walked over to speak to them. They asked if they could have a job, helping with the harvest. "We need a bit extra money." Ben said they really did not need any more help pulling onions. The old people didn't say anything just, "Oh!" Their disappointment was evident. Ben said, "May I ask why you want a job dealing with onions?" The old lady said, "Our name is 'Stone' you may have know our grandson Peter Stone." Ben said, "Yes, I do remember Peter, he was a senior when I started school, but wasn't one of the school bullies." Mrs Stone continued, "He was in the 8th Army in North Africa. He had fought with the army from El Alemein to Tunis, driving the Germans and Italians before them all the way. He now is in Sicily. Before we left home to go in the army we gave him a tobacco pipe. It was very expensive. Now he has written and asked if we can send him another one. The one we gave him was broken when he was fighting the Germans. The price of the same kind of pipe is a lot more expensive, and we just can't afford it. That's why we want to earn a bit extra money. If we don't send out the pipe, and something should happen to him, we'll never forgive ourselves." Ben said, "There is a job in the sorting shed. Onions come in from the field and we have to bag them in twenty-five pound bags to meet an order from the American Army."

Ben was still in shock after Sarah had told him she had sold fifteen tons.

Mrs Stone said, "We are older, and don't expect to be paid too much."

Ben said, "You will be paid four shillings an hour, the same as anyone else." He asked them to start work straight away, which they did.

The following morning the Americans arrived as promised. Before loading the onions they unloaded one hundred pounds of jam, in two-pound tins, more than enough for everyone working on the crop to have at least two tins each.

Ben and Sarah continued selling to the Americans, and anyone else who wanted onions, until the last of the crop was sold. Despite the many anxious moments growing the crop, Sarah estimated roughly that they had many over £3,000 clear. Ben and Sarah didn't plan to grow that many onions again.

All the while, the onion saga was taking place, Ben and Sarah were still on call for air-sea rescue, but luckily there was no demand for their services. They had been out though, to the lobster traps.

David Bennett had heard the British Army was coming to town and, he asked Ben whether he knew about it. Ben hadn't heard about any army people coming and said, "There is activity all along the coast, preparing for the invasion of Europe, which would soon take place." David said to them all, when they were at the Carter's one evening: "When Tom told me that Britain would win the war, I asked myself: 'How?' The British had to withdraw from Dunkirk, brought home by a miracle from Dunkirk. The Royal Air Force won the 'Battle of Britain' against huge odds. The Germans thought their airforce was invincible, but Britain won. Britain was blown to pieces by German bombers. Britain endured the terror, and destruction, of their country when other countries would have given in. Now they were giving back to Germany, in good measure, what the Germans had handed out to the British, with bombers tearing up their country night and day. And now the British will go back with the allies and win the war, just like your father said it would be Ben. I'm so glad we came here."

Ben and Sarah often talked about Sweetwater Farm, where his grandparents had been so happy and content. There seemed to be an invisible magnet, which drew Ben and Sarah to the farm.

The British Army arrived a few days later. To start with they tore down the old sheds by the wharf, which had not been used for many years. They levelled the land, at low water, in the harbour. Concrete was laid down to form a huge ramp. The work went ahead quickly. A large shed was build at the top of the ramp. No one had heard anything but rumours about the army coming to town. No one tried to interfere now they were here.

The next week the landing craft arrived. More soldiers came to town and were placed in temporary billets.

The officers in charge started their training. They loaded the landing craft with soldiers, went out to sea quite a way, then turned and headed back and landed on the beach east of the harbour. The first few landings were not good, or very professional, but gradually, after doing the manoeuvre over and over again, they did become professional at it. The huge door in front of the craft would open as soon as it hit the shore. Soldiers would come out

134

quickly as possible and run up the beach in a short time.

The air-sea rescue continued to operate efficiently. The volunteers went to sea – including Ben and Sarah, two kids, who were fishers and had also driven the slick rescue boat.

An officer spoke to Ben and Sarah on the wharf. The soldiers were resting and were at a loose end. One asked Ben, "How many boats from Midhampton harbour went to Dunkirk?" Ben replied, "All of them, sir." The officer said, "I am interested in that boat over there at the wharf side." Ben replied, "That's our boat." The officer continued: "After, and during, the blitz of London the army was sent in to help dig people from the rubble and clean up afterwards, that is clear the roads where streets used to be. We were having a tea break, one day, and a soldier who had been rescued from Dunkirk spoke of a boat he thought was called 'Epsom Salts.' He couldn't really remember but, did remember that the boat was named after a laxative. I believe it was that boat, the *Syrup of Fig*. The soldier had told us of a boy who had been in charge of the boat that had rescued them. He even remembered how many men there were on the boat, and said 'eleven.' Was that correct?"

Ben said, "Yes!" The officer said, "Eleven men on that boat, and yourself?" "Yes!" said Ben. "Did you give them corned beef and beer?" Ben said, "Yes, sir." The officer said, "Well he wasn't making it up then after all, but no one had believed him." Ben said, "My father was going to go to Dunkirk, and had packed corned beef and beer on the boat. He broke his ankle, and I went in his place." The officer continued, "And you landed them just west of Dover on the beach. Then you had the long trip back here?" Ben said, "Yes, sir."

Sarah, who was more easily provoked when the subject was mentioned, interrupted and said, "He is never going to do anything like that again." The memory of Ben leaving for Dunkirk was always on her mind. She burst into tears.

The officer said, "It is a miracle that you ever got home, but you took part in a far greater miracle: 'The miracle of Dunkirk.'"

The officer walked slowly back to his men. He said, "That boy took that boat," pointing to the *Syrup of Fig,* "to Dunkirk and brought home eleven men. Don't ever let me hear any of you complain again." Several of the soldiers present had been brought back from Dunkirk, and knew the conditions that Ben had had to deal with.

The soldiers continued to prepare the landing craft for the operation of swarming up the beach.

Ben and Sarah took the *Syrup of Fig II* out to sea. They was no emergency but the coast guard had been warned to have a boat out at sea, in case aircrew needed them. American and British planes were now concentrating on targets in France. They were preparing for D-Day.

No one knew what others areas on the South Coast of Britain were involved with, or doing. Everything was TOP SECRET.

The *Syrup of Fig II* sailed, at moderate speed, about three miles out. There was no activity for Ben and Sarah to be involved in. Sarah scanned the surface of the sea, just in case there might be someone out there.

She was looking almost due west and saw a large fish jumping in a small area and asked Ben what kind of fish they were. Ben took the binoculars and watched the fish play for a while. He thought they might be dolphins, but he had never seen anything like them. He didn't really know what they were. He watched for a while and then he saw the reason. There was something floating in the sea, causing the fish to behave as they were. Slowly Ben and Sarah took the boat to the black object that the fish were jumping over. They realised it was a sea mine. Ben stopped the boat and called the coast guard telling them the position of the mine.

Ben said that they should inform army personnel, in case there were more mines out there. If one of the landing craft had struck a mine the casualties and loss of life would have been terrible.

Sarah continued to scan the surface of the sea and she spotted two more mines. The coast guard was called again with the news.

Ben and Sarah were told to anchor the *Syrup of Figs II* and not move. The reason given by the coast guard was that there was a lot of metal making up the *Syrup of Figs II*, that could draw the mines toward it, if they were magnetic mines.

The coast guard said, "We have called the Admiralty, and they have a minesweeper already at sea. There have been mines laid in several places along the coast. The minesweeper will not be with you for about two hours so you will have to stay where you are until she gets to your position. Keep an eye on the mines and don't get close to any of them. If you are needed for rescue, the boat in the next harbour will look after the problem. A lifeboat has been launched as well, to take your place." Again the coast guard said, "Don't move – just stay where you are. The Navy will be in contact with you soon. They will be using the same wavelength as we are – keep your set open."

There was no sound other than the usual static from the radio. Eventually, after what seemed like hours, a voice came from the radio asking the question, "Where are you, *Syrup of Figs II*? Other ships in the area and their men said, "The navy has 'indigestion'." Sarah answered the radio saying. "The *Syrup of Figs II*." The reply came, "The RAF have nurses at sea to administer it."

Sarah said, "We are due east of you. We can just make

you out."

Minesweeper: "How many mines can you see?"

Sarah: "We have three here, and we are in the middle of them. When you see us, you will know were the mines are."

Minesweeper: "Can you tell what kind of mines they are?"

Sarah: "All I can tell you is that they are black, and look horrible."

Minesweeper: "I expect they are magnetic. Do NOT move or go near them – will be there in a few minutes – there may be more mines just below the surface – we can detect them if they are there."

The soldiers were waiting on the pier watching. They had a radio set, and were listening to the ship's radio. A soldier remarked, "Where that rescue boat is anchored is the route we normally take."

The minesweeper slowed right down. They were seeking mines methodically, back and forth. The radio on the *Syrup of Figs II* came to life again. The minesweeper reported, "There are three mines we can see. There are four more we have picked up a position on, but cannot yet see. *Syrup of Figs II* stay where you are – don't move – you are right in the middle of a small minefield, and very lucky not to have hit one. We are coming in very close to you and will get you out of there."

Slowly the minesweeper came towards them, still scanning the sea. The minesweeper looked quite large as it neared the *Syrup of Figs II*. More orders came from the minesweeper. "Follow us out of here, keep fairly close behind and you'll be okay." Ben was reminded of the paddle steamer as he moved along behind the minesweeper.

They had moved about half a mile from the mines. Minesweeper: "We are going to explode all we can find here, and then we will see you home. There will be large explosions. But don't worry. Anchor again now and wait. It will not take too long."

There was gunfire from the minesweeper and the first mine blow up with an enormous explosion. They blew up the others visible to them. They fired, as Ben and Sarah said, later some sort of missile to detonate the four they had not seen.

The minesweeper now said, "We are going to see you home. Then we will sweep the whole area. Come behind us as you did before."

Ben was told to anchor again as the minesweeper swept the mouth of the harbour. The radio came on again. "All's well. You can go home. Thank you for your co-operation."

Sarah replied, "Many thanks."

The soldiers were still waiting on the pier as the *Syrup of Figs II* sailed into the harbour, and gave them a cheer as it anchored and was tied up.

Rose nearly always watched the sea when Ben and Sarah were out there. She heard the explosions, which shook her home, and she was filled with relief when she saw the *Syrup of Figs II* come into the harbour. She said to herself, 'Will the war never end?'

Ben and Sarah came home and they were both exhausted from their ordeal. Before any landing craft went to sea again, the minesweeper came to check for mines.

After they had rested, Ben and Sarah went to the Bennett's home. They too had heard the explosions and were worried, as Rose had been. David and Ruth were not in their usual mood. They had heard that the Russians had overrun parts of Eastern Europe, where there were concentration camps.

David and Ruth were terribly upset saying: "The Germans have been killing our people. The Jews are being rounded up and killed. Not because they had committed any crimes just because they were Jews. How could a nation of so-called civilised people produce such vile monsters?

"Relatives and friends we had in Germany have been rounded up. If we had stayed there we would have no doubt been murdered too."

Neither Ben nor Sarah knew how to respond. Ben said, "How I wish the war would be over soon."

David went on, "When Kennedy was ambassador here, he said: 'The Jews deserved what they were getting. He is just as wicked as any German. I am sure he wanted Britain to lose the war. No wonder Churchill had him sent back to America."

David and Ruth changed the subject. They asked how the crops were growing etc. Ben replied, "The growing season is almost over. We have Brussels' sprouts to pick and cabbages to harvest, but not much else." David said, "You and Sarah are happy together aren't you?" They replied together, "Yes, we are!" and Sarah added, "And will be forever."

Sarah escorted Ben to the door and asked him if they could go to Sweetwater Farm the following Sunday. She continued, "After recent events I would like some peace – and expect you would too."

Ben left for home. His parents had been worried since the mine explosions. Ben said he was sorry that he hadn't let them know he was all right, and Sarah too of course. They said Rose had told them already – so they knew.

Ben went to his room almost as tired as he was on his way home from Dunkirk.

The following Sunday, Ben and Sarah informed Rose and their parents that they were going for a picnic. They took the same route, as before, looking down on the farm.

Nothing seemed to have changed much. The beauty of the place impressed them just as much as the first time they saw it together. They walked to the stile and then along the path to the lake. There was a slight chill in the air. It was late autumn and most of the leaves had fallen from the trees, but the large beech trees were still clothed in golden leaves. Where leaves had fallen onto the land around, the land was golden too.

The reflection of the gold on the smooth water of the lake made it look magical.

They didn't make love as they had last spring. They sat and enjoyed the food they had brought with them and enjoyed the peace. It was hard to believe a war was raging not too far away. There was no sound. Just a few days ago huge explosions from the magnetic mines being blown up took place.

Ben lay back and slept a while. Sarah picked her way around the lake, seeing her reflection in the smooth water occasionally. She walked back to Ben and decided they would have to leave.

Perhaps when the war was over they could enjoy longer moments of peace. They took the same path as before. They were almost by the farm when Mr Fulton, the owner, spotted them coming across the field. He came out of the house to see them and was pleased that they had come round again. He asked them into the house as before. He enjoyed their company.

Ben and Sarah accepted tea, which was offered. Mr Fulton had heard that the Germans had mined the harbour entrance, and of the part Ben and Sarah had played in finding the mines.

After some light conversation he said, "We have decided to sell the farm!" and added, "I know you would like to live here and I would like to see you have the farm. I don't think two youngsters of your age would have the funds to do so." Ben replied, "We most likely would be able to buy the farm if the price was reasonable."

Mr Fulton looked from one to the other, wondering if Ben was joking. They were not joking. He asked them what they considered reasonable.

Ben replied, "What ever the farm would sell for at auction."

Mr Fulton thought for a while, and then said, "Very well, very well. I will sell the farm at auction. I will get what the farm is worth, and you will pay no more than it is worth. I'm sure my wife would agree to that." Mr Fulton still could not understand how two young people like Ben and Sarah could ever think of buying the farm, let alone pay for it. They were too young to get a mortgage, and no bank would lend that amount of money to a couple of youngsters their age. Mr Fulton promised to let them know when the farm would be sold. Ben and Sarah left.

As they made their way back to their homes – Sarah asked Ben if he thought they really would have enough money to buy the farm. He replied, "I'm really not too sure. It depends on how much the farm makes." The next question, "What are we going to do if we do buy it?" Ben said, "Get married, I suppose." Sarah said, "You haven't asked me yet." They both smiled at each other. Ben said, "I never doubted that we would get married. However…" he said to Sarah in a serious manner, "Sarah Bennett will you marry me? We could become officially engaged on your birthday in the spring." Sarah replied, "Thank you! I have been waiting for you to ask me that for nine years, ever since the time you gave me that rose when we first met. We will keep our promises of marriage to ourselves though." Ben agreed.

By late 1943 the battle of the Atlantic was over. Some ships were torpedoed by U-boats. The Americans were arriving in Britain in great numbers, as were the

Canadians, some straight from Canada and some brought back from Italy. The campaign in Italy had taken men from many countries.

The bombing of Germany continued to destroy the German cities, as they had done to Britain. The Russians were advancing from the East. Germany was losing the war but still fought hard. Everybody expected the invasion of Europe to take place from England.

The Germans sent the Buzz Bombs, unmanned aircraft with a huge bomb in them. Once again London bore the brunt of the latest onslaught.

There were some celebrations for Christmas. Ben felt awkward about it as Sarah's parents didn't celebrate Christmas but treated the day as a holiday. Ben and Sarah exchanged gifts. Ben had good reason not to make too much of Christmas Day.

The Bennett's and Sarah came to dinner at the Carter's, and everybody enjoyed it, under the circumstances.

The air-sea rescue was active, but with less demand for their services, despite the increase in air traffic.

The RAF, American and other people were involved. Some crashed and rescues were made.

Ben and Sarah saw Mr Brooks less now than when he had started teaching them. They told him about Sweetwater Farm, and how they would like to buy it. Mr Brooks was pleased. He had started the two off, the studying and investing in the stock market, to help teach them maths. This had developed into an operation, far longer than he could have foreseen. Their investments had grown. Mr Brooks, when asked by Ben, how much the investment was worth, told them 'roughly £23,000', without the money from the onions, which they had just invested.

Ben and Sarah were beyond being pleasantly surprised. They were elated. Ben thought, and said, "That will be enough to buy the farm." Mr Brooks understood that they had to keep the matter of the farm purchase to themselves. He told them that they would start selling their investments when the farm was advertised for sale. The money received when the time came was to be paid into Ben and Sarah's bank account. They would have liked Mr Brooks to share, but he refused.

A week later, after more discussion about their stocks and shares, Mr Brooks advised them that they should start selling them. His explanation being that if there was a dip in the stock market they might just put the farm purchase in jeopardy. As the shares were sold their account grew over the following weeks. Even the bank manager acknowledged their existence when they came to invest money on a fairly regular basis. They had not, by any means, reached halfway in selling their shares when they passed the £10,000 figure. They continued selling until Mr Brooks announced that there was enough. There was still a lot to sell, and perhaps they had sold enough to purchase the farm. Their account now showed over £22,000. Ben and Sarah agreed.

In early June the Home Guard was put on full alert. They knew D-day was not far away. The soldiers stationed in the area were well trained and fit.

More landing craft arrived, filling up the harbour and only leaving enough room for the local boats and the air-sea rescue to depart and return. The town seemed to be overrun by British Army personnel who were accepted and treated well by the local inhabitants. A few eventually married local girls and came to settle in the town after, the war was over.

On June 5th all the soldiers were ordered to board the landing craft. More landing craft were coming down the coast. More ships were visible along the coast since the Dunkirk evacuation. The landing craft left the harbour and joined the armada already at sea.

In the morning the sea was empty of ships of any kind. The planes, which had towed over the gliders and dropped the airborne soldiers, were returning home from France. D-day was a busy day for Ben, and Sarah and the rest. Some planes, mostly DC 3's, were running out of fuel and others, badly shot up, were landing in the sea.

Air-sea rescue boats were very busy all day. Some lifeboats were launched along the coast, a service admired and respected by everybody for the bravery of their crews, over the many years. They were masters of rescuing people from the sea under terrible conditions.

By evening June 6th the BBC broadcast that a beachhead had been established in Normandy.

The Germans had been expected to land some troops in England to cause havoc, and perhaps to hinder a lot of the Allied troops going down to France. But that never happened.

Ben and Sarah were on call for twenty hours, as were the rest of the volunteers from the 5th June, and stood down when demand for their services lessened.

Canadians, British and Americans were ashore at Normandy. It was hard to imagine that the soldiers who had been in Midhampton training were now in the battle.

Within a few days an airfield had been established in Normandy and planes were already making use of it.

Mr Fulton, owner of Sweetwater Farm, came to see Ben as he has promised to do, when he and his wife had decided that they would definitely sell the property. Neither Rose nor Arthur saw him come or go luckily. Ben and Sarah didn't want anyone to know that they might try and purchase Sweetwater Farm.

Mr Fulton said the completion of the sale would be

late autumn, when the new owner would take over the farm and move in. The auction would take place most likely in late August. He would let them know the date when the auctioneers decided. Ben and Sarah had a lot of discussions about the process of an auction, farm auction or otherwise. In fact they had never been to an auction. They wondered if they would have difficulty getting an auctioneer to accept bids from them, as they were so young. They decided to ask for advice and help from the lawyer who had advised them and completed the sale of their field, and ask if he would manage the legal side of the purchase of Sweetwater Farm.

They decided to go and see him, and went to his office to make an appointment. The appointment was made for the following afternoon. His secretary took them into his office. The lawyer was pleased to see them, asked them to sit down, and looked at them expectantly, wondering why they wanted to see him.

Ben started nervously talking first and then asked the lawyer if he and Sarah purchased more land could he please manage the legal side of the purchase for them. The land was going to be auctioned and they needed advice on how to proceed. The lawyer had not heard of any land for sale, and asked where the field was that they wanted to purchase. He had no doubt in his mind that they could purchase another field. Sarah spoke, "We hope to buy Sweetwater Farm, which used to belong to Ben's grandfather." The lawyer stood up from his chair fairly quickly and paced the floor in the small space behind his desk. He said, "But how? That farm will make a lot of money. I doubt if you can find enough money to buy it. What does your grandmother think about the purchase?"

Ben said, "She doesn't know, and mustn't know until the farm is bought." Again the lawyer had doubts in his mind about what he was hearing. He liked the young couple, he had seen them often, and had heard a lot about them. They were fine young people – but that didn't mean they could afford to buy the farm. He was thinking, 'how can I let them down without hurting their feelings?'

After a few minutes he said, "Yes, I'll do what you ask of me when the time comes." Ben could see the old man was uncomfortable and full of doubt, so Ben handed the lawyer their bankbook showing they had just under £24,000 in their account.

Sarah said, "We didn't show you the book to 'show off,' and we really expected that you would have doubts about us purchasing the farm, but we are very serious about purchasing it."

The lawyer asked how they had amassed such a fortune. Ben told him. The lawyer said, "How I wish you had included me in your dealings." He then added, "You two people are remarkable. I think that amount should be more than sufficient to buy Sweetwater Farm."

Ben and Sarah left the office and walked to the harbour. Sarah suggested that they go out to the lobster traps. "It's a day early, but maybe there will be a catch." They went out in the *Syrup of Figs*, and hauled the traps.

The catch was surprisingly good. On the way home, they stopped the boat, let her drift and fished for mackerel. They caught enough for both families, and for Arthur and his wife.

They talked about what they would do if they managed to get the farm. Ben said they could no longer go fishing, as they had done for years. They couldn't keep farming the field where every square foot was already cultivated. The flock of hens would be moved to the farm. They would grow their own grain and would be able to keep more hens. On the lower land of the farm, they could grow anything they wanted to grow in the way of crops.

Ben said, "I wonder if Arthur would like to move back

147

to his old cottage. It had been renovated and modernised since he lived there, and is much improved since he last saw it." Sarah was thoughtful. The way of life they had known and enjoyed would be no more. Then she thought of the little lake in the woods, and the beautiful farmhouse and its location, she decided she wouldn't forgo that opportunity.

They were content and happy to go back to the harbour and deliver their fish. The lobsters were well cooked, and still warm when they were delivered.

Arthur asked them in for a cup of tea, which they were pleased to accept. Ben casually remarked, "Do you ever miss your cottage at Sweetwater Farm?" Arthur and his wife spoke together, "What we wouldn't give to go back there. The happiest of our days were spent there."

Ben and Sarah had their answer. They made their way home, but on the way called into the barn. They walked together to the sacks of grain, and then made love. They sat for a while and then made their way back to the Carter home.

The war was at last going well for the Allies. Soon it would be over. More concentration camps were liberated – camps of murder and death. The Bennett's knew they would never see their family or friends again. The German monsters had killed them.

In May, the Germans surrendered. The war was over. Everyone celebrated. The church bells rang for the whole of the day. The terrible ordeal was over.

Sweetwater Farm was well advertised in the local papers, to be auctioned on the 8th July 1945. Ben and Sarah obtained an order to view the farm from the auctioneers. They walked to the farm, and this time Mr Fulton knew they were coming. They met his wife for the first time. She took Sarah over the house. She had thought it a waste of time, but showed her just the same. Ben talked to Mr Fulton, while Sarah was looking at the house. Mr Fulton put the same question again to Ben, "Do you really have the wherewithall to purchase the farm?" Ben replied as before, "If the farm makes a fair price then I might have a chance."

Mr Fulton told Ben that there were other people coming to see the farm, as they were, and that they seemed fairly prosperous people. The people arrived before Ben and Sarah left the house, and came in to be introduced by the Fulton's, who told them that Ben's grandfather used to own the farm.

The newcomers were full of themselves to the point of being rather arrogant. They asked Ben what he did for a living and when told him that he grew vegetables he offered Ben a job on the farm after he had bought it. Ben laughed and refused.

Ben was also surprised at how sure the man seemed about buying Sweetwater Farm. Ben and Sarah excused themselves from the house and thanked the Fulton's for asking them, and for explaining the boundaries of the farm to them.

The newcomers, who were so sure they would be the ones who would buy the farm, asked if Ben and Sarah were in the habit of walking around farms that were put up for sale.

Sarah replied, "No – only this one." Ben could see she was getting very angry and got her away. Sarah said, loud enough for all to hear as they walked away, "What a conceited jackass."

Ben and Sarah headed for the woods and the lake. The food they had brought with them was enjoyed, up to a point. Sarah was still angry at the arrogance of the people they had just met. For a while they didn't speak, just sat there deep in thought.

Sarah broke the silence. "We will have to sell all the

stocks and shares we have and be prepared to use the other savings we have as well. I am determined that we buy Sweetwater Farm. People like those two we just met should be made to work in a pigsty."

The day was warm but they didn't swim. They were there to view the farm, and that is what happened. As they walked they almost ran into the couple that were so sure they would buy the farm. They walked into every field belonging to the farm. They were well pleased with everything they saw. They left for home.

The air-sea rescue service was disbanded. The *Syrup of Figs II* eventually left the harbour and all the volunteers who had operated the boat saw her leave. They all had different stories to tell of the various rescues they had made. Rose, Arthur and his wife were there. The day was fine, and Ben asked them out on a trip in the *Syrup of Figs*. They jumped at the invitation. Ben untied the ropes holding the *Syrup of Figs* to the wharf as they climbed onboard.

Meg jumped aboard and took her usual place. The engine started, the Norton 500cc had never let them down. Slowly they left the harbour, heading out between the piers. Ben increased speed and turned the boat east.

He looked for the beach where they had picniced before and where he had spent the night, when he came home from Dunkirk. They landed as before. They sat and chatted about various subjects. Rose brought up the news about Sweetwater Farm being sold. They talked for quite a while – Rose, Arthur and his wife. Ben and Sarah bursting to tell them that they planned to buy the farm. Rose said, "I wish I had enough money to buy it back. For my last years, I would like to live there again." Arthur and his wife agreed. Arthur said he was thankful to have had the opportunity to have helped Ben and Sarah despite having to live in town. They all started for home, having enjoyed their trip.

The next day Ben and Sarah went to see the lawyer about the handling of the affairs, that is, if they bought the farm. Ben asked the lawyer if he could be present at the auction, which was to take place the following week. The lawyer agreed.

Ben said there might be a problem bidding for the farm, as he and Sarah were rather young – and Ben didn't want anything to happen that would hinder their bidding.

Mr Brooks sold the last of their stocks and shares. The total now was over £30,000 in the bank.

The bank manager was puzzled. He was a short fussy man who strutted about the bank ready at all times to deal with less fortunate people who needed money. He would grudgingly lend money as if it was his own, and not the bank's. His way of lending was as if he was doing the customer a great favour, and then charging an interest rate, which helped his wages.

Ben and Sarah transferred most of the money in their savings account to a cheque account that they had just opened. The teller informed the manager, who strutted around from his office, and asked Ben and Sarah what they were going to do with the money. Ben and Sarah had told no one that they intended to purchase Sweetwater Farm. They certainly were not about to tell the bank manager.

Ben said, "We are going on a world cruise." The manager was angry. He knew no cruise ships were sailing until the wars end. He foolishly said, "I can stop the cheques you sign." Ben, quick off the mark, said, "You cannot stop us from transferring to the other bank in town." The arrogant attitude of the manager changed immediately. He said, "Oh, of course I would never stop any of your cheques – the bank will help you any time." Ben and Sarah did not like him at all.

Rose, who had had a cough for some time, gave the doctor cause for concern when she went to see him about it. He went in to see the Carters. He said, "I suggested to Rose that she do no more than necessary – and that she rest. I think she has pneumonia – in fact I am sure. I'll try to persuade her to go into hospital. With the new drugs we have now her problem can be cleared up quite quickly – but not if she will not rest." The suggestion that she do as the doctor said, made by Ellen, didn't help much. It took Ben and Sarah to persuade her. Rose reluctantly agreed and went by car to the hospital, quite upset. They took her to the room where Sarah had been when she was so desperately ill and nearly passed away. Rose saw no sense in going there, but soon settled down. She knew she wasn't well.

The doctor started treatment at once – and gave her a sleeping pill to make her rest.

The date of the farm auction had come. Ben and Sarah went along to the saleroom as planned, walking from their home. They called at the lawyer's office on the way. They all walked together to the large hotel in which the auction was to take place. It was a large room, used for weddings and other functions. Chairs were set out in rows, facing a low stage. Several people were there already. A few were interested and some just there out of curiosity. Ben, Sarah and the lawyer sat almost at the back of the room. The lawyer reasoned that from there they could keep an eye on things.

Sarah spotted the couple they had seen when they went to look over the farm. The man looked arrogant and confident.

The auctioneer entered the room with his entourage. He shuffled his papers for a while. The room was now packed with people. The auctioneer tapped his gavel, and then spoke, "We are here today to sell Sweetwater Farm –

if you haven't particulars they will be passed to you. The successful bidder will be required to pay a 10% deposit now, and the remainder on completion of the sale – the date is one month from now."

Ben and Sarah could hardly contain their excitement. Ben could feel his heart pounding and Sarah looked at him nervously. The lawyer was pleased that he had come with them.

The auctioneer started the bids on the farm. The first bid came from the man they had met at the farm. In quite a loud voice he bid £8,000. This was quickly followed by a bid from a guy in front. He bid £8,500 – then £9,000 – then the bidding moved slowly up to £14,000. The lawyer whispered to Ben, "Off you go." Ben held up his hand saying, "£14,500." The auctioneer hesitated, and then asked Ben if he was bidding. Ben said, "Yes!" The auctioneer remarked, "You look rather young." Ben's lawyer stood up and said, "I can guarantee that the bid is genuine."

It had been wise for them to ask the lawyer to be present. Several people turned to see whom the bidder was, including the man Sarah had taken such a dislike to at the farm. He looked quite explosive. The auctioneer continued, "I am bid £14,500 for Sweetwater Farm,"followed by a bid from the man Sarah disliked for £15,000. He had bragged that HE was going to buy the farm. Ben then bid £15,500. There was a pause in the bidding – then the auctioneer offered to take £100 bids. £15,600 from the man, who was now a lot less confident. Ben bid £15,700.

"£15,800," bid the man. The lawyer whispered to Ben, "He has not got much left – you bid £16,000." The man was beaten. The auctioneer tried for more. He made the usual speech: "If there are no other bids I shall sell. Going once. Going twice. Going three times. The farm is sold to the young man almost at the back. What is your name?"

Ben replied, "Benjamin Carter and Sarah Bennett."

Several people applauded. Ben and Sarah were well known. They sat for a while as the room cleared of people. A few people walked over and congratulated Ben and Sarah. The man and his wife that they had met on the farm both glared at Ben and Sarah as they left.

The lawyer was delighted. "Now we go and pay your deposit, and I will take things from there. There is one thing that you have to do, get your grandmother's signature." Ben said, "But she is in hospital." The lawyer said, "Then we will have to go over to the hospital." They paid the £1,600 deposit, and the lawyer said he would complete the business within the thirty days. Ben and Sarah signed the agreement to purchase. The lawyer said he needed Ben's grandmother's signature, and unfortunately she couldn't get here today. "I will have the agreement to purchase co-signed by her and here in a short time." "Will one of you come with me," he said to the auctioneer. The auctioneer was a bit surprised, but agreed. They drove to the hospital in the auctioneer's car. They then walked to Rose's room. She was fast asleep. Ben woke her gently by tapping her arm. She awoke and looked around and gathered herself together. She saw the men in dark suits. She asked if they were undertakers adding, "If you are – you've come early." By now she was wide awake, and knew something was up. Ben told her they needed her signature, "the same as when we bought the field." "Have you bought another field," Rose asked.

Sarah said, "No – we have bought back Sweetwater Farm." Rose closed her eyes – she must be dreaming – she had dreamed so many times of being back at Sweetwater Farm, always waking and feeling disappointed when the dream was not true.

Ben said, "We REALLY HAVE bought the farm…" The auctioneer butted in, "Yes, they have bought what they say, the youngest bidder I have ever had for a farm."

Rose co-signed the agreement to purchase with Ben and Sarah, tears of joy running down her cheek.

Ben and Sarah left hospital and went back to tell their parents. The Bennetts had been discussing returning to German to try and claim the property they had left in their hurried departure from Leipzig. They arrived at a decision. They would not return home to their old home. They were happy and safe in England. Their shop prospered and most people accepted them. The thought of leaving Sarah behind if they went back to Germany was the biggest reason <u>not</u> to leave. They knew she would never leave Ben. It was settled.

Ben and Sarah came into the Bennetts' shop looking excited and very happy. The Bennetts' could see something was afoot. David remarked to them and said, "You two look happy – you must have received good tidings or something."

Sarah blurted out, "We have bought Sweetwater Farm." The Bennetts' said, "Well done, but <u>how</u> did you pay for it? What did you agree to pay?" Sarah said, "£16,000, we saved all for it. Its ours – no mortgage – no rent – completely free of debt." The Bennetts' were shocked, to say the least.

"There is one more thing," Ben said. He looked at David and Ruth, who were still in a state of shock after hearing about the farm purchase – "Can I have your permission to ask Sarah to marry me?"

Sarah didn't know that Ben had planned to say such a thing. She had thought about it. Ben had spoken of getting married one day – but now they would be. They were going to get married – no matter what!

The Carters' knew also that they would always be together. Mr and Mrs Bennett knew also that they would always be together. They both said, "You have our blessings." You have already been blessed by a power stronger than ours. How long have you been together?" Sarah said, "Nine years. We both knew when we first met – that there would be no one else for either of us, we have been through many things together, good and bad. Nothing will change our minds."

Ruth asked, "Where will you get married, in a church or in a synagogue?" Sarah said, "Neither. We will be married at the Registry Office, that way no one will be offended or embarrassed." David said, "Who will give the blessing on the marriage?" Sarah said, "Ben and I have been blessed for nine years already." The Bennetts' never mentioned leaving England again.

Ben and Sarah left, and went to see Ben's parents. They had already heard about Ben and Sarah buying Sweetwater Farm. They congratulated both of them.

Tom and Ellen had not heard that they were getting married, but it wasn't a surprise to them. They were pleased, but couldn't imagine their lives without Ben and Sarah.

Ben and Sarah now left the Carters' for Arthur's home. They were having a meal when Ben and Sarah arrived. Ben broke the news to them both. "We have bought Sweetwater Farm." There was silence. Arthur's wife thought, 'this is a very poor joke to be played on us.' Arthur asked, "When?" "At the auctions this afternoon," Ben said. Arthur said, "How did you buy it?" "We bid for it – the same as the others did," Ben said.

They wanted to believe Ben and Sarah, but couldn't understand how two youngsters like these could possibly buy a farm a big as Sweetwater Farm.

Ben had the receipt in his pocket for the deposit he paid on the farm. He showed them both. Eventually they both understood – the youngsters had really bought the farm. Then Ben told them the other news, ""Sarah and I are getting married." This was too much for Arthur's wife. She grabbed her cup of tea and upset the whole lot. They all laughed heartily. Then she said, "Perhaps we can go home." She looked enquiringly at Ben, who said, "Yes, we are all going home. Your old cottage has been modernised and is really nicer than when you left it. We can go over and see it if you like to, but we'll have to walk." In a matter of a few minutes Arthur and his wife were ready to go.

They all walked fairly quickly, Arthur telling Ben what they would do when they were back farming Sweetwater Farm. "Perhaps we could have a herd of South Devon cattle back."

Ben smiled and said, "We'll have to wait and see." They walked into the empty farmhouse. There was 'silence,' as if the house was waiting for them. They walked over to the cottage. There too there seemed to be a feeling of welcome. Arthur and his wife went from room to room. Each one had a happy memory.

On the way home they went into hospital to see Rose. She was very pleased to see them, and still very excited. She said she was ready to go and wanted to leave right away. Ben and Sarah persuaded her to stay in hospital, but if the doctor was agreeable they would take her up to the old farm the next afternoon. There was no need to wait for the completion day, in September, of the farm deal. There was no mortgage to arrange, or any other legal hindrance.

Ben and Sarah married the same day the farm sale was completed. They planned to spend their first time together on the farm. They were married at the Registry Office as planned, and made their way from the Registry Office to the hotel, where they used the same room for the reception that had been used for the auction. There were no formal invitations sent, but everyone who came was welcome.

The former coast guards, air-sea rescue people, all the

fishermen, who had boats in the Midhampton harbour who had been to Dunkirk, who had worked so closely with Ben and Sarah throughout the war, were at the reception.

Unknown to Ben and Sarah, Tom Carter had been writing back and forth to the men from Penzance, since they came to the harbour seeking fuel on the way home from Dunkirk.

Tom had written, telling them that Ben and Sarah were getting married, and giving them details. They both spoke of their meeting with Ben on the way to Dunkirk. They wished Ben and Sarah great happiness.

Mr Brooks toasted the young couple, and marvelled at their achievements.

Rebecca came from London, where she was still working for the Red Cross. She had an emotional meeting with David, Ruth and Sarah, with whom she had escaped Germany.

It was a very happy and moving occasion. Ben gave Sarah a gold chain with the Star of David to wear as a necklace. The star was big enough to contain small red cubes in the shape of a rose.

Sarah gave Ben a package, which Ben thought was a picture. Sarah had framed some of her neat writing she copied from the Old Testament. She had printed:

Thy God will be My God
Your ways will be my ways
Whither thou goest, I will go
And I will walk in thy footsteps
All the days of our lives.

Ben was deeply touched. They left for their home and for their honeymoon at 'Sweetwater Farm.'

The end!